I0664870

HER OTHER FAMILY

a novel

Edward A. Dreyfus

Enchanted Villa Press

LOS ANGELES, CALIFORNIA

Enchanted Villa Press
Pacific Palisades, California 90272
www.edwarddreyfusbooks.com

Publisher's Note: This is a work of fiction. Names, characters, places, and incidents are a product of the author's imagination. Locales and public names are sometimes used for atmospheric purposes. Any resemblance to actual people, living or dead, or to businesses, companies, events, institutions, or locales is completely coincidental.

Her Other Family/ Edward A. Dreyfus
ISBN 13: 978-0692826829
ISBN 10: 0692826823

Dedication

This book is dedicated to all the courageous adoptees who seek to find one or both birth parents. Their journey is not simple or easy, churning up many dormant or long buried questions, the answers to which, often alter their life.

Preface

The shadow is a moral problem that challenges the whole ego-personality, for no one can become conscious of the shadow without significant moral effort. To become conscious of it involves recognizing the dark aspects of the personality as present and real. This act is the essential condition for any kind of self-knowledge.

Carl G. Jung

All human personality contains a light and a dark side. No matter how moral a person may think he or she is, there is another part of the personality that is immoral. Our task is to find a balance between these two forces, not by repressing one in favor of the other, but by fully acknowledging both. If we repress our darkness, it is likely to seep out in subtle ways or, in some instances, make its appearance in full force, rocking our foundation. We often hear about people doing things that are quite out of character for them. We hear about the quiet, polite young man who goes on a rampage or the church-going, proper woman who suddenly kills her husband.

A repressive society is more likely to drive people to deny or ignore the dark sides of their personality. Rather than protecting us, however, this approach leaves us more vulnerable and susceptible to unexpected and confusing

5

eruptions resulting in out of character behaviors, thoughts, and decisions.

The antidote to such potential eruptions is to bring the darkness into the light, making the unconscious conscious, and creating a balance.

In *Her Other Family*, we accompany Marianna Bolton on her journey to discover her birth father's family. She moves from the lightness of her life to the darkness of life on the streets of New York and, in the process, she finds herself going on a more important internal journey of self-discovery.

CHAPTER ONE

Marianna Bolton, a 28-year-old struggling actor, physical trainer, nutritionist, and animal rights activist sat in an old Adirondack chair, drinking her Sunday morning latte, while browsing through a recent issue of *Variety*, the magazine devoted to the entertainment industry. As she thumbed through the magazine, she came across a small ad. Reality Productions was looking for participants for a new documentary featuring adults adopted as children who had never met one or both birth parents. The ad caught her attention.

Marianna rarely thought about her adoption. She knew that her mother became pregnant with her when she was seventeen years old. The big surprise came when Marianna turned eighteen; her parents told her that she had been adopted as an infant by the man she had always known as her father. She'd always assumed that he was her biological father and that her parents simply had married young.

Marianna remembered the day she'd learned the truth. Her parents, prompted by an article they had read about adopted children often not knowing their true family medical history because they didn't know they were adopted, revealed to her that that the man she knew as Dad had adopted her at birth. Her mother explained that Marianna's biological father disappeared shortly after her mother became pregnant. Marianna recalled being stunned by the revelation. She had a visceral memory of the feeling even now, as she thought about that day. It was quite jarring to learn that for eighteen years the man she had known to be her father was not biologically related to her. But after the initial shock wore off, she realized that it didn't make much difference. After all, her Dad was, well, still her dad. He was the one who had taken her to school most mornings, taught her to ride a bike and how to drive a car. He had earned the title of Dad.

She recalled her parents telling her that, when they told their own parents they were pregnant and getting married, they never discussed the identity of the birth father and the birth father never knew of the pregnancy. They believed there was no reason for their parents to know the entire truth, so they let them think the child was his. In fact, Marianna's adopted father's name, Victor Bolton, appeared on her birth certificate; that's all that mattered. Hence, her mother and her mother's husband were always Mom and Dad; they were her parents. The picture of her mother being pregnant with some other man's baby while still in high school and her parents being teenagers when they married had quickly faded from Marianna's mind to be replaced by a narrative of young love.

Marianna remembered asking a few questions about the circumstances and how uncomfortable her mother was in relaying the story. Her guilt over becoming pregnant as a teenager was still palpable eighteen years later. The story her mother told her was that she had gone to a party, had too much to drink, and ended up having sex with a twenty-one-year old college senior by the name of Tony Donatello who attended college in New York. Marianna tried to dig a little deeper, but there was very little more her parents could (or would) tell her about her birth father.

She made a small effort to locate her birth father on her own by searching the internet websites for locating ancestors and missing persons, but came up empty-handed. As far as she was concerned, that put the matter to rest; she'd had no further interest in finding her birth father.

Nothing more about it had been said since that day almost ten years ago. That's just the way the Boltons were. Anything of import was just swept under the carpet. The idea of sharing feelings was foreign to them. They were strictly a meat and potatoes family, both literally and figuratively.

From all appearances, they were a typical family of three. In truth, however, Marianna did not know much about her mother's history, the circumstances of her pregnancy other than the part about getting drunk at party, or the nature of her parents' relationship. Though she knew her mother had had a totally hysterectomy due to complication s during her delivery, she didn't know why her father married her mother when he was only eighteen or why they didn't adopt another child. These were issues that no one ever discussed. And, until now, they'd held no real interest for Marianna. Most of the time, feelings were simply buried in typical Bolton style and the Bolton family, as is true for many families, seldom complained about anything.

Mary and Victor Bolton relished the simple life. They would never stand out in a crowd. They attended church, had participated in the Parent Teachers Association when their children were young, volunteered in community activities, hung an American flag on their porch on Veterans Day, the 4th of July, and any other patriotic holiday. They were as American as apple pie. They would never say an unkind word about anyone. They did not want to draw attention to themselves lest their secret be discovered. Theirs was a typical 1950s-television family. But, for Mary and Victor it was their life; they lived it. For Marianna, it felt constricting. But she quickly learned that making waves would only upset her parents. She loved her parents so, at least within the family, she conformed to their style.

Now, on thinking about her history and remembering how surprised she was about learning that she was adopted, Marianna couldn't help but wonder what other secrets her parents held. *Were the circumstances of her mother's teenage pregnancy the only Bolton secret?* she wondered.

While the information about her origins didn't significantly change the family dynamic at the time, reflecting upon it now did change how Marianna perceived her family. She began to think of them as secretive, non-communicative, and inauthentic. This was the first time she had the thought that things weren't the way they appeared to be. She sipped her latte and stared at the blue sky, musing. She listened to the dogs barking in the distance, the wind in the trees, and watched the hawks glide lazily in the sky.

The magazine ad was just the nudge she needed to look deeper into her origins. She decided to apply for the show. As an actress and as an adopted child, she thought this might be an opportunity both to learn about her ancestry and to showcase her acting abilities. The way she thought about it was she would have an opportunity to talk with people in the business and perhaps network a bit for other acting gigs.

At the very least, it would be an adventure. She felt excited. She smiled as she picked up her cell phone.

Marianna called the number listed in the ad, expecting to leave a message since it was Sunday. However, much to her surprise, someone answered. She was told that she should submit her story in writing, giving as much detail, including, background information on her missing parent as she could find. If her story sounded compelling enough, they would contact her.

When she told her husband, Grant, about her intention to participate in the documentary that might lead to her discovering her birth father, he had some reservations. Grant was a very methodical engineer. He was disciplined in all areas of his life tending to weigh pros and cons of all decisions and very deliberate in everything he did. Marianna was more emotional and more prone to deal with the world on an intuitive basis. Their different styles were complimentary, making for a good balance in their marriage.

"Are you sure that you want to open up that can of worms, babe?" asked Grant.

"What do you mean, can of worms?" inquired Marianna.

"Well, it may not be a fairytale ending," replied Grant speaking softly. "Your birth father could be a druggy or alcoholic. Or he may not want anything to do with you."

"Yeah, but at least I will know," said Marianna. "Now I know nothing about that side of my life."

"Be careful about what you wish for," said Grant. "If you do find him, it could change your life. Are you sure you want that?"

Marianna nodded, taking in Grant's comments.

It was a genuine inquiry, no judgment. Grant would support Marianna no matter what she decided. That was just his style. He loved her. And it was the nature of their relationship. Marianna and Grant gave each other lots of room to be their own person and pursue their own direction.

Mariana made up her mind to continue with her participation in the documentary. She set to work on collecting all the bits and pieces of information she had surrounding her biological father. She had his name, new his approximate age, where he went to school, and that he had friends in the suburbs of Seattle where her mother lived. She wrote all of this down and set if off by email to the address she had been given.

A few days later she received a reply stating that she was being considered as one of the participants in the documentary and that the producer would like to meet with her. An appointment was set up for the following week.

Joseph Pendergast, the producer for Reality Productions, was a casual sort of guy, quite unassuming, and wore a baseball cap, t-shirt, jeans, and tennis shoes: a typical, twenty-something young filmmaker, energetic and personable. He smiled warmly when they met, shaking Marianna's hand as he ushered her into his small, windowless office. It was obvious that Reality Productions was not exactly a big budget production company. Marianna immediately felt comfortable with him.

Joe found Marianna to be an introspective and transparent young woman. That made his job that much easier. The facts that she was both attractive – at about five-two, with straight, dark hair, penetrating green eyes, with an athletic build – and an actress were a bonus. She would be comfortable in front of a camera and easy to look at. He told Marianna what they were looking for, explaining that they wanted the show to be an in-depth look at what people experienced when they meet a parent or child with whom they had no prior contact. The show was not intended as a fluff piece. All participants would have to be fully transparent and have all their reactions filmed for later airing on national television. They even had a professional mental health counselor available to participants to help them process their feelings. Joe explained that meeting with a long-lost parent could be quite unnerving, even traumatic. He told her that he had been adopted as an infant. He learned of his adoption as a youth and had always been curious about his biological mother. When he found her, she was married and had a family. She wasn't interested in having him become a part of her life. It was a difficult time for him, but as he came to learn, not an uncommon experience for adopted children. It took him years to come to terms with this. He knew first hand, from his own experience and that of other adoptees with whom he had connected while in support groups over the years, that adopted children, upon finding their birth-parents always went through an emotional struggle. Marianna appreciated Joe's candor.

He further clarified that there was no guarantee that, even if they found her birth father, he would want to appear on the show.

Marianna was impressed with Joe's sincerity and desire to present a serious piece on family reunification. She gave him as much background information as she could, along with samples of hair follicles and saliva for DNA testing. Joe explained that the show had a team of forensic investigators that would use all the information she had given him as the basis for an all-out search for her birth father. They would comb the entire United States using every bit of information she could provide, schools, names, addresses, and friends and acquaintances.

When she left the audition – which was more of an

interview than an audition – Marianna felt good about the experience. As with all auditions, however, she knew she would have to wait for the call-back. She knew that it was a long shot that they would locate her birth father and even more improbable that he would agree to meet her once his genetic identity was established. Marianna knew most of the time the call-backs never came and normally it didn't much matter. She hoped this time would be different. This time it was not a character she would be playing; this would be about her. She would be the star.

As she drove home, she could feel herself becoming even more curious about her ancestry. It was strange that it took an ad in a newspaper to spark her curiosity. Now, at twenty-eight, she was very curious on multiple levels.

While telling a friend about her experience with the audition and sharing more information about her adoption, the friend told her that, at least from a legal perspective, her mother was raped. Statutory rape, her friend (who happened to be an attorney) told her, was any act of sexual intercourse between someone under eighteen and a person over twenty-one. It didn't matter whether the minor consented or not.

Marianna had never thought about it. *Maybe she was raped! Not statutory rape, but actual rape. I don't know.* Now she was developing more questions that she wanted to ask her parents. But she decided to wait until after she met her birth father – if and when this happened. In typical Bolton family tradition, she kept the entire audition and concept for the show a secret from her family. *I am as bad as they are*, she thought. But she rationalized it by thinking that, at this point, she didn't even know whether she would be accepted as a contestant for the show even if they could locate her birth father.

It's strange, Marianna thought, *how little I know about my parents, who they are, their relationship – nothing really personal. I never asked them much about themselves. Am I different from most people? Do other people ask about their parents? Do people want to know their parents? Do parents want to be known?* She remembered a friend of hers who sat down with a tape recorder with her father when he was dying in the hospital. She had wanted to know all about his life and how he became the man she knew as her father. *Is that what it takes? Someone dying before we want to truly know them?* These thoughts stayed with her as she waited for the call-back.

Several weeks after the audition, Marianna received a call from the producer, Joseph Pendergast, telling her that that they had located her birth father and he was willing to participate in the project and have their meeting filmed for the show. From the time she volunteered to be in the documentary, meeting her birth father was simply a possibility. Now it was real. She was almost as taken aback at the prospect of meeting her birth father as she had been upon learning from her parents that he existed.

Once again, she debated whether to tell her parents that she was about to meet him. She believed that it would be upsetting to her mother and wondered whether her father would feel threatened by her birth father coming into her life. She thought he might wonder whether she would feel more connected to him than to the man who'd raised her. Neither of her parents was particularly self-disclosing or psychologically astute. Everyone in her family protected everyone else from knowing things they imagined would be upsetting which was one of the reasons they kept secrets. She was raised a Bolton and, thus, had adapted to their secretive ways. She decided to wait. At least for now, this would be her secret. She would first meet her biological father, see what happened, and then decide when to tell her parents. She was glad that the actual showing of the program wasn't going to happen for several months down the road. It would have been difficult to keep the secret if the program was being aired live.

As the days leading up to the filming went by, Marianna reflected on her family and what she knew about them. She knew her mother had had an affair or relationship with a man several years older than her and became pregnant. She knew that she was adopted at birth by the man whom she always thought was her father and that her parents, at least initially, had not told their own parents that Marianna was not conceived between them. They had led both sets of parents, as well as all other relatives, to believe that Marianna was conceived by the two teenage-parents and that the pregnancy was the reason they married so young. She did not know when or if her parents decided to tell their parents the truth. Was it at the same time they'd told Marianna? Did her grandparents even know?

In addition to these questions for her parents, she had many more to ask her birth father. And she was certain that, after their meeting, she would have many more.

CHAPTER TWO

O n the first day of the filming of her meeting with *bio-dad* (which was how she had begun to think of him), she could feel the tension. She rarely was nervous before an audition, but this time was different - big time. It was not simply an audition for a part in a movie; this was real. She was about to meet her biological father; just the thought of it took her breath away.

She arrived at the television studio where the film crew awaited her. They shadowed her, recording each nuance of her reaction and the meeting to follow. Marianna was led to a sound stage that was set up to look like a living room. There was a couch, two upholstered chairs, a coffee table, and a rug connecting them all. When she arrived on the set, she stopped dead in her tracks. She felt her heart rate increase and a slight film of perspiration form on her palms. Seated in one of the upholstered chairs sat forty-nine-year old Tony Donatello, an olive-complexioned man with wavy black hair and green eyes – just like hers. Upon seeing Marianna enter the set, he stood up, a wide grin on his face. Marianna's eyes widened. He was short of stature and possessed an athletic build. The similarity between them was striking.

His eyes sparkled on seeing her and he smiled warmly. "Oh-my-god!" exclaimed Tony with wide-eyed enthusiasm. "I can't believe it. You look just like me!"

Marianna stared at him. Despite her best efforts to contain herself, she felt her eyes well up with tears and her bottom lip trembled slightly.

"This is unbelievable," she said, barely above a whisper.

The camera caught every emotion, though Marianna was oblivious to everything going on around her. The set was as quiet as a crypt.

Marianna and Tony sat down on chairs facing each other. They started talking at the same time.

"It's strange," began Marianna. "Once, a long time ago, someone asked me about my nationality. I told them my mother was Italian and my father was Swedish. This guy said, 'Swedish? Really? Have you looked in the mirror lately?' I never gave it much thought until my mother told me of my having been adopted by my father. But then I forgot about it – until now."

Tony chuckled. "No, Marianna. If your mother is Italian, then you're a thoroughbred Italian."

"Now I know why I love Italy and Italian cooking so much. I even learned Italian. It must be genetic. Like an Italian gene," joked Marianna.

They both nodded as they laughed.

"Why did you decide to audition for this show, Marianna? Were you looking for me?" asked Tony, looking directly into Marianna's eyes. She found his green eyes penetrating - almost pleading. He wanted to hear that she had been looking for him. As a boy, he was not ready to be a father; but the years since changed him.

She wasn't sure how to answer, so she decided on the truth rather than giving him what he wanted to hear. "I wanted to find out more about my ancestry. For most of my life I thought of my parents as the bearers of my full medical history. But that was a myth; a convenient lie. The show gave me the nudge I needed to get that information." She paused for a moment and then asked, "Why did you want to meet me?"

Everyone on the set held their breath. Tony spoke softly. "Until I received a call from Joseph, I didn't know you existed. I didn't know I had a child in the world. In fact, I didn't think I could have children." His voice cracked.

Tears filled Marianna's eyes. She noticed several members of the stage crew wiping away tears as well.

This was quite a revelation for Marianna. Her mother had not told her this, leaving her with the impression that her birth father did not want anything to do with the child that was on the way. Now he was telling her that he simply hadn't known she existed.

Tony told her that he was pretty wild when he was in college and had slept around quite a bit during those days. He indicated that none of the girls ever told him about a pregnancy. He said that he hadn't kept in touch with any of the girls he had fooled around with and that he couldn't remember her mother.

Marianna reached into her handbag and retrieved an old picture of her mother pregnant with her. She showed it to Tony.

"Does this picture jog your memory?" she asked.

Tony took the picture and held it in both hands studying it carefully. He shook his head. "No. Sorry. I don't have any memory of her." He handed the picture back to Marianna, looking into her eyes as he did so.

There was a momentary silence before the conversation picked up again.

Marianna and Tony went through a few magical moments of getting to know one another, including sharing photos on their smart phones of themselves and family members from years gone by. Much to her surprise, Marianna's eyes once again filled with tears. The resemblance between herself and other members of Tony's family was striking. *This could be – is – my family,* she thought. Initially believing that Tony had simply abandoned her mother when she was pregnant, Marianna wanted to be reserved and guarded with him. But she found it difficult to contain herself. He was so warm and responsive; so unlike her father. She found herself feeling drawn to him.

She learned that he was a construction worker, living in the San Francisco Bay area, married for twenty-five years to the same woman, and, ironically, had adopted her child, who was two years old at the time they'd married.

What a coincidence, thought Marianna. *Both of my fathers had adopted their wives' children.*

After they completed filming the episode, Marianna and Tony agreed that they would keep in contact through texting, email, and Skype. Marianna did not know what to do with what she had learned from Tony, especially about his not knowing her mother had been pregnant.

She left the studio even more confused than she had been before meeting Tony. Something was not right. Someone was not telling the truth. Her parents told her that her mother had had a fling with Tony and ended up pregnant. *Or did they? Did my parents actually tell me that story, or did I make it up? Is that the story I wanted to believe? Funny thing about memory,* she thought, *we can tell a story so often that we end up believing it. Is that what the psychologists mean when they say we all have our own reality?*

As much as she wanted to rush home and confront her parents with this new information and tell them about discovering her biological father, she had reservations. She wanted to become better acquainted with Tony and the rest of his family – her family. And she feared that telling her parents about him would both disrupt her relationship with them and interfere with getting to know Tony. *Maybe there's a reason why families keep secrets? But who does it benefit?*

CHAPTER THREE

O ver the course of the next several weeks, Marianna and Tony engaged in many conversations, texts, and several video chats. They began a spate of daily texting back and forth. The emails and texts were filled with sharing. Marianna looked forward to each communication. She checked her cell phone regularly, responding immediately to each announcement of a new email or text from Tony. She and Tony were discovering one another, much like a couple dating, but they were doing it remotely and digitally. Marianna could tell they both enjoyed the process, looking forward to the next text or chat. For Marianna, not only was it fun to discover her birth father, but Tony seemed so revealing and was willing to be vulnerable with her. It was quite a contrast to her father's stoic, taciturn way. She had always wanted to have a more intimate relationship with her father, Victor, but that simply wasn't his style.

Marianna knew that if she and Tony were to become part of each other's lives beyond the first few weeks of getting to know each other, their respective families would have to contend with an intruder. This would cause an upset in the status quo, that familiar feeling that comes with predictability. But once the introductions took place, all that would change and nothing would ever be the same again. Therefore, Marianna was cautious, always trying to consider the outcome before acting. Or at least, that is how she thought of herself.

She saw herself as a deliberate, thoughtful, careful, and considerate person.

For his part, Tony was quite excited about discovering that he had sired a child. He'd raised his wife's child since she was two and had even adopted her, but to find that at forty-nine years of age he had a biological child of his own took him over the top. He had learned when he was in his early thirties that he was not likely to have children due to a very low sperm count; he wasn't one of the lucky ones able to still impregnate a woman despite a low count. Marianna was, to his knowledge, his only biological child.

Marianna, on the other hand, was more curious than excited. She already had a father and was not looking for another one. But Tony presented more than just DNA: he brought with him another set of relatives. This meant uncles, aunts, and cousins. She was particularly interested in them. They were blood. She had minimal interest in his wife and daughter; they just came along with him as part of the package. Her other family was the big draw. Discovering a bunch of Italian relatives intrigued her.

Marianna wanted to share her concerns about the impact that their relationship might have on her parents and on Tony's wife and child. But when she tried to discuss this with Tony, he virtually dismissed her concerns. He was convinced that it wouldn't be a problem. If Tony believed something, it was true.

"Tony, you don't get it," she began during one of their Skype sessions. "Your daughter can't help but feel threatened by me. I'm blood and she's adopted," Marianna reasoned.

"No, she will be excited to meet you. She'll have a sister; it will be great," said Tony, as if, by convincing Marianna, he could will it to be true.

"And your wife - as welcoming as she might want to be towards me for your sake," said Marianna, "she is going to feel far more protective of her daughter. You can't force me on them, Tony. It will have to be on their terms."

"No worries," replied Tony with a smile. "You'll see."

"And what about my parents?" added Marianna. "How can you be so sure that they will be okay? After all, you're my birth father. Don't you think that might threaten my dad?"

Tony paused, but only for a moment. He ran his fingers through his hair. "They're adults. They can handle it. They'll be happy for you. I'm certain."

For Tony, everything was simple. Nuances escaped him. He was impatient to have his wife and daughter meet Marianna and that's all there was to it. But when he broached the subject with them, they did not seem quite as excited about the prospect as he had hoped. Marianna had been right.

When he told Marianna what happened when he spoke with his wife and daughter, he acted irritated and disappointed. However, Marianna was quite sympathetic to their view. She knew that she was the interloper and potentially could disrupt their comfortable family unit. *Why would they be excited to meet me?* she thought. On the other hand, she did want to spend more time with Tony and learn more about her history and her extended family. And she knew that this could not be done in secrecy. To do so would be like having an affair.

Similarly, Marianna had her own reservations about telling her parents about meeting Tony. She knew that it would be upsetting to them; especially to her mother. She always perceived her father as the steady one; nothing ever seemed to disturb him. She believed that he would just accept Tony as bio-dad: a sperm donor and nothing more. But her mother could become emotional. Marianna perceived her mother as fragile; not particularly empathic or introspective, but definitely emotional. She didn't want them involved - at least, not yet. She was enjoying developing a relationship with Tony and didn't want her parents' feelings to disrupt the process. *This is about me, she thought. I have always put their needs ahead of my own. This time it going to be about me.*

Marianna talked it over with her husband Grant, who was generally very supportive of his wife. He tried to caution her to move slowly, not only because of her mother, but because he wasn't certain that her father would be as easy or accepting as she imagined.

One afternoon, as Marianna and Grant sat in their farmhouse kitchen having a cup of green tea, Marianna told Grant about her most recent conversation with Tony and her thoughts about her parents' potential reaction. Grant held his cup of tea with both hands. "I know if I were in your dad's position, I wouldn't be comfortable."

"Why?" asked Marianna. "My dad's my dad. He's the one who raised me. No one is going to take his place." She could feel herself getting defensive. She placed her hands on her hips, a stance she developed as a child – defiant.

"Yeah, I know that," replied Grant calmly speaking in measured tones. "But as you've said all along, your dad might feel threatened. Tony is blood. You share DNA with him." He paused, put his cup down, took Marianna's hands in his, and looked her in the eyes. "Hey, babe, I know you are confused.

There's a part of you who wants to tell your parents and there's another part that is afraid of how they will react. All I'm sayin' is that, as a guy, there's a good chance that your father will feel threatened. Like you said: you look like Tony, not your dad."

Marianna remained quiet. Her defensive posture melted away as Grant spoke. Her arms dropped to her sides. After a moment, her head gave a slight nod of acknowledgment that Grant might be right. After all, it was no different than what she had originally thought. She would have to give a lot more thought to her approach with her parents.

Marianna loved Grant's "calm under fire" disposition. He rarely got angry; his emotional band-width was narrow, never overly happy nor overly sad – he lived in the middle zone. Marianna, by contrast, could become really angry and really down; not bi-polar, but with a wider emotional range. Most of the time it worked out fine between them. Occasionally, however, she wished he would show a little more emotion. Sometimes she thought he was boring and she felt the desire to shake things up. Everything about him was subdued. Even in bed, she thought.

Eventually, Tony's wife, Dawn, sent Marianna an email introducing herself. Marianna and Dawn began to email each other. Tony's daughter Jane joined in the emailing. The conversations were polite and understandably somewhat formal. This was new territory for all of them and there were no guidelines on how it was to go down. They talked about the coincidence of both Marianna and Jane being adopted as children by men who did not raise children of their own and whether Jane had any interest in learning about her bio-dad. She learned that Jane's father had died in an auto accident and she had no memory of him; she had contact with both sets of grandparents, but given that Tony had shown no interest in or connection to his own family, she had no interest in learning more about them either. As far as she was concerned, they were just people in Tony's previous life.

At one point, they began to talk about a potential visit from Marianna. Jane expressed her desire to meet Marianna. They were each struggling to get their heads around the idea that they were stepsisters. Jane said she couldn't help but wonder if blood was thicker than water. She acknowledged that she felt a bit weird, given that she had spent twenty-five years thinking she was Tony's only child only to find that he had a biological daughter. Although she was curious about meeting Marianna, Jane also had major reservations.

Marianna wondered whether her own mother would be as protective of her as Dawn seemed to be of Jane. Marianna knew that her parents always viewed her as independent. Being the only child born to very inexperienced young parents, Marianna quickly learned that she was going to have to become independent and take care of herself. Marianna grew up learning to take care of her parents, rather than the other way around. She became the perennial caregiver, never asking for anything from anyone. She was defiantly independent and self-sufficient. Even as a child, she would seldom allow anyone to help her. It was a family joke that even at three years old, with her hands on her hips, she would always be saying, "Marianna do it 'self!'"

This added to Marianna's reservations about talking with her parents. She wondered whether they would even recognize that she might need their support in discovering her birth father. And if she did ask for it, would they be able to give it? She was not willing to take the chance. She could feel her perception of her parents changing. It was confusing to her.

One day Marianna received a text from Tony stating that he and Dawn had decided that they wanted to visit Marianna. Rather than wait for Marianna to decide upon dates to visit him, he would take the initiative. He offered her a choice between two dates. He told her they would be coming down for a vacation and planned to spend time with her. Marianna felt herself getting pissed. *How could he presume to intrude on her space and give her two dates to choose between without discussing whether visiting her at this particular time was convenient?* she thought. She was also pissed because he was dictating the terms. She felt that he was being too pushy, and she bristled. She hated when anyone would dictate terms to her.

Marianna thought it would be best to discuss the matter with Grant before she replied to Tony.

"So exactly what is it that you're upset about?" asked Grant, his eyebrows raised in curiosity.

Marianna stood in front of him with her hands on her hips. "What! Who the fuck does he think he is, deciding when he is coming to visit?" Her green eyes flashed.

Grant's hands went up in mock defense. "Whoa, babe. I'm not the enemy. I'm just askin'. You seemed to be going from zero to sixty in nothin' flat." Grant was always the voice of reason. His measured speech pattern soothed her.

She immediately calmed down. Grant had a way of centering her. Marianna prided herself on being rational and able to control her emotions. But when pushed, her fiery temper flared. She took a few deep breaths.

"The thing is," replied Marianna, constraining herself, "we've been talking about my visiting him up there. I've been feeling uncomfortable about going."

"Yeah, but did you tell him that? Does he know that you have reservations about going?" asked Grant. "Even I don't exactly know what those reservations are. And couldn't it be that he is just excited to see you?"

Marianna stared at him for a few moments. "I suppose you're right," replied Marianna, feeling mollified. At least temporarily. She couldn't stand anyone dictating what she should do and when. It was a hot button for her.

"What are your reservations, babe?" asked Grant. His voice was calm and soft.

Marianna hesitated for a moment. In a barely audible voice she finally said, "I guess I'm scared."

"You? Scared?" exclaimed Grant in feigned disbelief. "Now there's a first." He gave her a warm smile. "Wassup? What are you afraid of?"

"It's difficult to articulate," began Marianna. "Something just doesn't feel right. It just seems to be going too fast. You know me; I like to take things slowly. Deliberately. And here's Tony, all 'let's do it all now; everything will be okay.' Well, I'm not so sure. And then, without really hearing me when I tried to explain to him that I want to think more about planning a visit, he decides to just come on down and has the gall to offer me two dates as though the deal was set and all we had to do was choose a date." She could feel herself becoming agitated. "Well, fuck him!"

"I get it," replied Grant. "Why don't you give it one more shot. Tell him what you told me – but without the 'fuck him'." He chuckled. "And ditch the attitude."

Marianna smiled, relaxing her shoulders. She gave Grant a kiss. "Thanks, babe."

She went straight to her computer and tried to communicate her reservations to Tony, and her desire to slow things down. She told him she wanted more time to process their relationship and wanted him to take care of business in his family. She indicated that both Dawn and Jane were very friendly, but she knew they, too, must have reservations. She tried to explain to him that a meeting was a big deal for everyone and that she wanted them all to come to an agreed-upon date rather than having one forced upon them.

Much to her surprise, rather than being understanding, Tony lashed out in back-to-back emails, telling her that she was a troubled person who needed psychological help. He accused her of not being able to accept love even when it smacked her in the face. He reacted like a rejected suitor.

Marianna was totally taken aback by his outburst. Of all the possible responses she'd anticipated, this wasn't one of them. His reply deeply hurt and angered her, as well. She could not understand how he could be so malicious. How could he have changed so much? She wondered. Where the fuck did that come from? In a strange way, she also felt vindicated regarding her reluctance about visiting and her sense of discomfort.

"I'm glad I trusted my gut," she murmured to herself.

His outburst, though via email, was so intense that it shook something deep inside her. She couldn't put her finger on it, but it felt strangely familiar.

In the beginning, their relationship had taken off like a shot, like two people in the throes of falling in love. Daily contact, sharing, planning for the future - and then suddenly the bubble burst. Tony's explosion was abrupt and intense. As soon as Marianna expressed her desire to slow down the relationship, indicating that she was feeling overwhelmed and needed space, Tony became angry, like a lover whose affections were being thwarted, and lashed out, virtually destroying the nascent relationship. To her way of thinking, the intensity of Tony's reaction was unwarranted by both the duration and the nature of their relationship.

The unexpected disconnection from Tony left Marianna confused and angry. She felt seduced by his loving kindness, his warmth, and his ready embrace - and, of course, the promise of a large extended family. Being an only child in a small family, she had always wondered what it would be like to be in one of those big families she had seen in movies. She had begun to think that she would soon have Jane as a sister, once she could come to terms with Marianna's existence. Just when she was beginning to trust Tony and look forward to meeting his family, the rug was pulled out from under her.

She experienced his attack as nothing short of vicious and uncalled for, leaving her deeply wounded. Maybe, like Tony, she'd had more invested in the relationship than she'd believed.

Marianna then began wondering whether the Tony she had seen for the past several months was merely a façade, behind which lay the true Tony. She knew many men would put on a persona when in hot pursuit of a woman, only to turn into vicious, mean-spirited people once they captured their prey. Was this Tony? Marianna also believed that she would be able to detect such duplicity. *Obviously, I was wrong, she thought. And Tony is accustomed to getting his way and having things on his terms.*

This left Marianna with many questions. She recalled that, in one of their conversations, Tony had alluded to a nefarious past, especially when he was a young man. She recalled him saying that his father had Mafia connections. She also knew that her mother had met Tony when she was seventeen and became pregnant. Tony was four years older than her mother, making their sexual relationship statutory rape. She wanted to know more about their relationship and the real reason why her mother did not tell Tony about being pregnant. Marianna's adoptive father (aka Dad) was only eighteen when he'd married her pregnant mother. *What was their relationship? Why did her dad marry her mother and adopt Marianna? What did her grandparents on both sides think about these teenagers marrying and having a child?* Marianna didn't know where to begin.

She also had questions about Tony. *What was his past? What role did the Mafia play in his life? Was his father involved with the organization? Was Tony? Was there some kind of big family secret?*

Had it been anyone else, it would have been over. Marianna was not one to continue in relations once she spotted red flags. Yet, clearly, she was not quite ready to write Tony off.

CHAPTER FOUR

T he rupture in her relationship with Tony gave Marianna some time to think more deeply about what she wanted to do concerning her parents and telling them about finding him. She knew she had to tell them. She didn't like holding secrets. In fact, that was one of the issues that she and Grant had discussed early in their relationship. It wasn't that she felt it was necessary to share every aspect of her past with Grant; nor did she expect that of him. And she didn't expect that they should divulge confidences shared with each, by others. But she was adamant about sharing information that they each thought would be best not to share for fear of hurting or upsetting one another. She was fond of saying, "If you didn't want me to find out about it, then you shouldn't have done it."

But that applied to current situations, not necessarily to behaviors occurring before they got together - except in instances where the past behaviors might be relevant to their current relationship. She didn't want to find herself in the position of falling in love and then discovering that he had herpes or had a child or had been convicted of a felony or that he was a recovering drug addict. She figured there were enough issues to work through in a relationship without having to discover buried secrets to add to the mix once the relationship was under way. She expected full transparency up front giving each person a chance to part ways before being overly invested.

She believed that hiding things from one another was more damaging to a relationship than sharing and resolving issues early in a relationship. She remembered hearing somewhere that one of the reasons that people kept secrets was because they didn't want to have to deal with the consequences of the other person discovering the behavior or information. She believed that the often-heard excuse "I didn't tell you because I didn't want to hurt your feelings" or "I knew you'd be upset" was pure bullshit; it was always self-protective. In her experience, it was always easier in the long run to deal with the secret itself than to be discovered hiding something.

Marianna decided to begin with her parents. She thought it would be best to talk with them in person. So, she arranged for a trip to Oregon where they lived and planned to spend a weekend with them. She could feel her pulse increase in anticipation of the visit. She had no idea how they would react. Her parents, on the other hand, were just excited that they were going to see her. They had no idea that Marianna was on a mission.

When she arrived at her parents' modest home outside of Eugene, they both greeted her with open arms. Her father carried in her overnight bag and her mother and Marianna walked into the house hand in hand. Marianna was happy to see them. Her mother had prepared a snack and it was sitting on the kitchen table waiting for her. Marianna smiled. *That's Mom; always wanting to feed people. No one loved to eat more than Italians*, she mused.

After she settled in and they finished with the usual round of small talk, catching up during a short tour of the newly planted garden and the redecorated living room, they sat down in the kitchen for a cup of freshly brewed coffee along with the snack her mother had prepared.

Marianna's parents, Mary and Victor Bolton, were pleasant, conservative people who lived a modest, unassuming life. Marianna's mother was more talkative and generally more outgoing than her quiet, pragmatic, meat-and-potatoes father.

"There's something I want to talk with you about," began Marianna. "I auditioned for a documentary series and was chosen to be a participant."

Her mother's eyes lit up. "That's wonderful, sweetie. Congratulations," said Mary, turning her head toward her husband. "Isn't that wonderful, Vic?"

Victor Bolton nodded.

"What type of series?" asked Mary. "Like the Kardashians?"

Mary Bolton didn't keep up with the latest in television shows, but she did subscribe to People Magazine, so she had an idea of what was going on in pop culture.

Marianna hesitated for a moment. "That's just it, Mom. It's a documentary about people who were adopted as children and who want to find their birth parents."

Marianna's eyes flicked nervously from one parent to the other. Her father seemed to perk up. Her mother looked startled.

Marianna didn't know how to tell them, so she just blurted it out. "So they found my biological father, and I met him on the day they filmed the episode."

Her mother's face lost its color; her father leaned forward with his hands on his knees and looked at Marianna in silence.

"You met him?" asked her mother speaking slightly above a whisper. "In person?" Her cheeks turned slightly red.

Marianna nodded, averting her eyes. "Yes. I met Tony Donatello. And I've been texting and talking with him." She could feel the tension in the air.

On hearing the name Tony Donatello, both Mary and Victor Bolton stared at one another. They both remained quiet, not sure of how to reply. Hearing the name they hadn't heard for the last ten years – the day they told Marianna she was adopted – made them both swallow hard. This was a day they had hoped would never come.

"He was very warm and seemed quite pleased to meet me," continued Marianna. "He lives in the San Francisco Bay Area with his wife and daughter. It's interesting that he adopted his wife's child when she was two; she's now twenty-seven." Marianna talked quickly, trying to maintain an upbeat countenance.

Mary forced a smile. Her husband remained stoic, his face placid.

"What a coincidence," said Mary. "Did they have children together?"

"No. I think that is why he was so anxious to meet me," said Marianna. "Apparently, I am his only biological child."

Marianna's father shifted his position, jutting his jaw out. She knew he felt uncomfortable. She had seen him in awkward social situations before. His jaw was a giveaway. She turned toward him.

"Look, Dad; I know this might be awkward for you. But I want you to know that you're my dad; you are my father and always will be. Tony is – well, I have begun thinking of him as bio-dad. No one can replace you."

She placed her hand on his shoulder and smiled. Her father patted her hand and nodded his head, forcing a slight smile, in an attempt to assure his daughter that he was okay.

"Tony told me that he never knew that you were pregnant, Mom," said Marianna, turning toward her mother. "He said he was a wild kid, dated a lot of different girls. When I showed him a picture of you, he said he didn't recognize you."

Her mother played with the edge of the tissue she held in her hand. She tried to smile, but tears welled up in her eyes.

"That could be true. I never told him that I was pregnant," said Mary avoiding eye contact. "I didn't want that to be the reason he stayed – even if he wanted to – and I didn't want him to be involved in my decision to keep the baby. Uh - to keep you." Mary averted her eyes away from Marianna staring straight ahead. Victor kept staring at his wife.

Marianna sensed that something was going on between them that they weren't saying or not being truthful about. She already knew that her mother was pregnant before her parents married and that her mother was only seventeen at the time.

Turning toward her father, brows furrowed, searching her father's face for answers, Marianna asked, "Why did you marry Mom, Dad? You were only eighteen yourself. Why did you marry a pregnant girl?"

Her father looked up, his eyes filled with tears. It was a look that Marianna had never seen. "Because I loved her from the first day I met her in high school English. But she was always interested in older guys. So, we became friends. I just wanted to be with her." Victor looked at Mary and smiled. His face was a bit flushed with embarrassment.

He continued. "So when she told me she was pregnant and wanted to have the baby, it seemed like a natural thing for me

37

to step up and suggest that we get married. At first your mother was against the idea, afraid her parents would be angry at both of us. But I pointed out that if she told her parents she was pregnant by a stranger, they would be even more upset."

Her mother sat quietly, blushing. She began to tear the tissue she had been holding into small pieces. Tearing tissues was a habit she had developed when she was nervous.

The Boltons had been dreading this conversation since Marianna was a baby. While they hoped that it would never happen, they also knew that someday Marianna might want to locate her birth father. That was one of the reasons they had waited until Marianna was eighteen before even telling her that she was adopted. They weren't planning on ever telling her; but both their minister and their pediatrician had pressured them. The minister thought it was the right thing to do and the physician thought it was important that Marianna have accurate information about her full genetic history. She did not share her adopted father's gene pool. Her parents had been fortunate that Marianna did not seem to have any major illnesses during childhood where genetic information might be helpful; but they knew they were pushing their luck.

Her parents looked at one another and then at Marianna. They gave a collective heavy sigh and her mother began their story, this time the truth.

"When I was a teenager," her mother began, "I was, um, a little, uh, adventurous, you might say." Mary's cheeks flushed and she could barely look up from the torn tissue in her hand. "I hung out with a group of girls; one of whose brother was in college. He would invite us to parties when he was home from college during breaks. At one of these parties I met Tony." By this time Mary's face was crimson. Telling a daughter, even though the daughter was twenty-eight, about her sexual liaisons was not easy.

Marianna felt sympathetic toward her mother, who had always described her high school experiences and her life in general as quite traditional. She believed that her having sex with Tony had been her mother's only sexual experience which had, unfortunately, resulted in a pregnancy. Never did she expect that her mother had been even a little bit frisky. Marianna sat quietly as her mother struggled for the words to describe her meeting with Tony. *The longer the secret is held, the more difficult it is to share,* thought Marianna.

Mary continued. "When Tony asked me out on a date, I was thrilled. Tony was a college boy and I was merely a high school senior. We began seeing each other. You could say that I had a crush on him. We spent a few days together. Well, one night we went out to a movie. I told my parents that I was going out with a bunch of girlfriends. After the movie, we drove back to the apartment where he was staying with a friend. Tony attended school back east somewhere – New York, I think – and was visiting a friend out here on the west coast. Apparently, his friend had gone away for the weekend."

Mary hesitated. She looked at her husband, who gave her a small nod. And then she continued. "When we got to his friend's apartment, Tony turned on some music and poured drinks from the liquor bottle sitting on the kitchen counter. I wasn't used to drinking and immediately got a little drunk. We danced to the music." Mary hesitated again. "We ended up in bed." Tears flowed down Mary's cheeks as she recalled the events of that evening.

"Mom, did he rape you?" asked Marianna, placing her hand on her mother's.

Mary shook her head. "No. I wanted to do it. I thought – I thought I loved him. And I believed he loved me." Her head dropped. "I was such a fool." She wept silently; the tears rolled down her face. She tried to blot them with the crumpled tissue.

"I am so sorry, Mom," said Marianna placing her arms around her mother.

"The next day Tony left to return to school," added Mary.

"'Your mother didn't tell anyone what happened that night," said Victor. "Even I didn't find out about it until a couple of months later, when your mother told me she was pregnant."

"I never told anyone," said Mary. "I was too embarrassed. I blamed myself for just being a foolish girl who should have known better than to go off with an older boy I just met. I was stupid." Mary grabbed another tissue and began tearing it to bits. She was still blaming herself.

"When I found out about it, I wanted your mother to go find him and make him take responsibility," said Victor. "She refused. She didn't want anyone to know she had been so foolish. And she didn't want to have an abortion. We talked about that, as well. She was a good Catholic girl. Sex before marriage was a sin and abortions were even more sinful." Vic looked at his wife, his eyes moist. His love for her was palpable.

Mary had recovered somewhat, by this point. "Your father was wonderful. He was, and still is, my best friend. Despite what happened, he still loved me. So, we decided that being best friends would be a good enough basis for marriage. We didn't tell anyone about Tony and let them all assume that your father was the father of the baby. Once you were born, they did blood tests and other lab work, as is customary in case the baby or I needed a transfusion at some point; and some technician noticed that your blood type was incompatible with your father's - that he could not have been your father. The doctors, however, kept it confidential and your father's name appeared on your birth certificate."

Mary and Victor stared at each other for a long moment.

Marianna looked at them. Her eyes flicked from one to the other. "What? What? There's something you're not telling me."

"No one was supposed to know that I wasn't your biological father," began Victor. "But some nurse let it slip. Somehow your grandparents found out. We think it was some nurse commenting on what a nice boy I was for stepping up to marry this pregnant teenager, or some such thing. In any event, when your grandparents found out, they called a lawyer. The lawyer said that by law this was statutory rape. Tony could have gone to jail. But your mother didn't want to report the matter to the police. She just wanted to keep the baby. The lawyer suggested that for legal protection I should adopt you just in case there were complications later on. But, in order to adopt you, we had to get permission from the biological father; he had to consent to your being adopted."

"And that meant we had to tell Tony," said Mary. "The lawyer had an investigator find Tony at college and had him sign the papers giving up custody and parental rights."

"He couldn't sign away his rights fast enough," added Victor with a touch of disgust.

41

"So Tony *did* know you were pregnant after all?" exclaimed Marianna. "He lied to me!"

Now it was Marianna's turn to let out a heavy sigh. This was quite a bit to digest and process. *My mother fooled around, got knocked up, and my father adopted m -, fuck! I wonder why it never occurred to me to ask why my father's name appeared on my birth certificate? After all, I was eighteen when I found out I was adopted. I should have asked why he needed to adopt me if his name was on my birth certificate. Jeez!*

Then the topic turned to why her mother didn't want to report Tony to the police. There was a long silence. Victor looked at Mary before continuing. She gave him a slight nod.

Her father told her the rest of the story.

"Okay, the truth is once the investigators found Tony, and before asking him to sign the adoption papers, your mother and I went to New York and confronted him. Your mother told him that she was pregnant and that she wanted to marry him. Tony laughed at the idea. He had no interest in marrying her. And he had even less interest in being a father. He told her that if she ever told anyone about their affair, she would be sorry. He told us that he was the son of a big wig who was connected with the Mafia."

As soon as she heard the word *mafia*, Marianna's ears perked up even more. She thought of Tony's comment about having a dark past, and his father's Mafia connections. She then began wondering whether Tony remembered her mother when she had shown him the picture during the filming of the show. *For all I know, Tony could have been thinking about any number of other girls who could have been my mother, she thought. If Tony was a player, he easily might not remember my mother.* Marianna's picture of Tony took a decided downward turn. *I think he's a fucking liar. I bet he recognized my mother's picture. I bet the sonofabitch recognized the girl he knocked-up twenty-eight years ago!*

Her parents sat quietly, waiting to see how Marianna was going to react to their story. Marianna looked at them for a few moments before saying anything. Her mind was spinning. She then acknowledged what she understood them to be saying.

"An older guy whom you had a crush on impregnated you," began Marianna, looking at her mother. "When you and Dad confronted him, not only did he reject you, he threatened you." She turned to look at her father. "And you, Dad, you were in love with Mom and were her best friend. You married her and adopted me. Neither of your grandparents knew Dad adopted me. But both sets of parents, *my* grandparents, knew the whole story. Is that it?"

Her parents nodded at the summary.

Marianna shook her head in disbelief. "What a story," she said. "Are there any more family secrets?" She gave them a sardonic smile.

Her parents once again looked at one another. Another heavy sigh. They each nodded their heads.

Marianna was shocked. "You're kidding! There's more?"

Mary nodded. "Shortly after you were born," said Mary, "your father and I were approached by a couple of members of the mob. They told us your grandfather, Louie Donatello, Tony's father, knew that his son was your biological father. He wanted you to live with him. To this day, we don't know how Louie found out that Tony was your father." She paused.

43

"Maybe the investigator told him. Maybe Tony told his father. We just don't know."

Marianna's pulse quickened as she listened; her entire body was tense.

"But," continued Victor, "we weren't about to give you up. We were told that Donatello was willing to pay us to give you up. But we refused. We told them that unless they left us alone, we would tell the police that Tony raped your mother."

"You threatened the Mafia!" exclaimed Marianna in total disbelief. "Are you friggin' kidding me?"

Victor smiled. "We were kids! What did we know? Anyway, eventually we came to an accord: an agreement. They would leave us alone if we agreed never to press charges and never to tell anyone what happened."

Mary interjected, "And they told us that if we broke the agreement, they would…" She began to cry.

"They said they would hurt you," said Victor, finishing his wife's sentence.

By this time, Marianna's head was spinning – statutory rape, the Mafia – the vision of her pregnant teenage mother and father standing up to organized crime was mind-boggling. The thought that her paternal grandfather was a mob boss left her both awed and stunned. *My conservative parents were not so traditional after all – far from it. No wonder they're so secretive. Living with the threat of the mafia hanging over their heads would cause anyone to keep a low profile. Bio-dad's father was a gangster and perhaps so was bio-dad. And, the acorn doesn't fall far from the tree*, she thought as she recalled Tony's controlling nature and his outburst.

Marianna knew that she had to dig deeper. Despite not wanting to re-engage Tony in another round of texting, her curiosity about his past and meeting his mafia-connected family, was stronger than her anger toward him.

The rest of the visit with her parents went well. They had surprised her with their openness and acceptance; it was not what she had expected. She felt closer to them and appreciated their candor, love, and support as she continued her journey to discover more about her biological father. She felt sympathetic towards them, imagining the ordeal they must have gone through as teenage parents dealing with an unplanned pregnancy and the threats. She admired her father for his courage, commitment, and love for her mother. Not many men, young or old, would have wanted to marry a woman who was pregnant with some other man's child. And then adopting and raising that child at only eighteen years of age; that was impressive. Marianna looked at her parents' relationship in an entirely new light.

Marianna felt relieved after talking with her parents; she imagined they felt relieved as well – no more secrets. She was glad that her father didn't feel threatened by her desire to get to know Tony and perhaps even his entire family. Now that she knew more of the backstory to her parent's relationship with Tony, she was even more motivated to hear Tony's side of the story. She wanted to confront him with the lies.

She knew that once the show aired, there might be further questions, and some suppressed feelings might re-surface, especially once they saw Tony live on screen.

But for now, all was good.

CHAPTER FIVE

The flight home was uneventful, but Marianna's mind was busy. She ruminated on what her parents had told her; especially the part about Tony lying to her regarding his interactions with her mother and saying that he hadn't known that her mother was pregnant. She believed he also lied about not recognizing her mother's picture. Marianna hated liars. She wanted to rip him a new asshole, but she knew that if she did, any chance of connecting with the East Coast family would be lost. *Gotta keep my eye on the ball,* she thought. *But why?* she wondered. *Why is meeting Tony's family so important to me? I know it is; I can feel it, but why? Curiosity isn't enough of a reason for upsetting my comfortable, well-organized, and predictable life. I should leave well-enough alone.* But she knew herself better than that; she wasn't about to let go what could be the adventure of a lifetime. And it wasn't just a trip to Adventureland; it was her life. She remembered that people more often regret the things they didn't do rather than the things they did. She did not want to have regrets. *But is that enough of a reason? All I know is that this is something I must do.*

By the time she returned home to Los Angeles, Marianna had decided that the next time Tony contacted her, rather than ignore him, as she had been doing, she would reply. She had many questions; mostly about his history and the relationship with his father, in particular. She also wanted to see whether he would acknowledge having raped her mother. She wanted to talk with his wife and daughter, Dawn and Jane, to see whether they knew anything about Tony's past and whether they had contact with his gangster father. She was curious about whether they ever experienced Tony's dark side both in terms of underworld activities and in terms of personality.

When Marianna arrived home, she found Grant puttering in the yard. She wanted to tell him about her visit with her parents. Marianna and Grant had a strong relationship. They were best friends, lovers, and business partners. He often brought a refreshing point of view to their conversations and she relied on both his creativity and pragmatic approach to projects. It was a fine counterpoint to her tendency to bring more emotion and intuition to situations. Where she had a tendency to focus on details, Grant was a big picture kind of guy. He played the long game, where she reacted more from the gut. Marianna wanted his perspective on both her parents and Tony.

She walked over to him and sat herself down in one of the Adirondack chairs near where he was puttering.

"Hey, babe, welcome back," said Grant, seeing her from the corner of his eye. "Have a good trip?"

"Yeah, it went a whole lot better than I expected," replied Marianna. "Got a few minutes? I'd like to tell you about it and get your input."

"Sure, no problem." Grant stopped what he was doing, removed his work gloves, gave her a kiss on the forehead, and sat in the chair next to her. "What's up?"

Marianna went through the entire story about her parents, Tony, and her grandfather.

"Wow, that's one hell of a story!" said Grant, eyebrows raised with a look of mixed surprise and wonder spreading across his face. "A Mafia grandfather! Yowza! *Bio-dad* Tony is the son of a Mafia boss, committed statutory rape and impregnated your mom, his father threatened them and you, and Tony lied about knowing your mother was pregnant with you, right?"

"Yep, that's pretty much it," replied Marianna with a slight smile. "I'm mob-connected," she jested. "My parents kept it a secret as best they could in an attempt to protect me. Overall, they were far more candid than I expected. Now I'm left with what to do about Tony. I'm still pissed at him from the last go-round of texts, but rather than not talking to him, I want to confront him with what I've learned. And, I must admit, I am very curious about the rest of his – my – family, and *la cosa nostra.*"

Grant nodded. "I get that. It is not everyone who can say that their grandfather is a Mafioso kingpin. And I get that you want to confront Tony about his lies – your mother and whether he knew your mother was pregnant. But, this could be like opening Pandora's box. You don't know what kind of stuff could come out. The Mafia is not a group you want to rile up. They're like a hornet's nest. You already saw how Tony exploded over nothing. And he says he left the organization twenty years ago. Can you imagine how your new grandfather might react? Or other family members?"

Marianna sat quietly for a moment, considering what Grant said. She was conflicted. She knew her impulse was to throw caution to the wind and proceed full steam ahead. But she'd learned over the years to respect Grant's more analytic approach.

"I suppose you're right," said Marianna, "but I can't shake the desire to rip Tony a new one for lying to me."

"I get that," replied Grant, wiping his brow with the back of his hand, "but what if he didn't lie? What if he was telling the truth? What if he didn't know about his father threatening your parents? The question is whether you want to stir the pot by bringing up the Mafia connection. Maybe you should let sleeping dogs lie."

"Maybe I'll just deal with the lie and not the issue of his father's threat," replied Marianna, looking away from Grant at some distant flower in their yard.

Grant looked at her with a smirk. "Yeah, right; you're going to talk to him about knocking your mother up and lying to you without mentioning the threat from the *Don Mafioso.*"

Marianna just looked at him. She knew he was right.

"Well, you've got my opinion," said Grant, reaching for his gloves. "Now it's up to you. You'll do whatever feels right to you. And, as usual, I'll back you up, whatever you decide." Grant smiled the smile that always comforted her and went back to his gardening, leaving Marianna to contemplate her next move. He knew that she needed time to mull over her options, and she needed to do it alone.

It wasn't too long before Marianna heard from Tony, despite her having told him that she wanted some space from him. She knew that he would not honor her wishes. His irrational explosion meant little to him. It was just a matter of time before he contacted her. This time she was looking forward to it.

He had already shown that this relationship was all about him and his desire to control its progress. She wondered whether this was a characteristic of his. She wouldn't be surprised, given his behavior and what she imagined about his history. She was curious about how both Dawn and Jane saw him. That was another thing – Marianna couldn't imagine him being honest with her. There were only three options, as she saw things. One, he was pretending to be Mr. Niceguy with them, and they never saw his dark side; two, they were complicit with him and his underworld activities; or three, they were completely dominated by him. An Option Four never occurred to her.

This time she answered her cell phone when Tony called. He seemed to be surprised that she'd answered. He began the conversation by telling Marianna that she'd misinterpreted his comments. He tried to explain that what he had been trying to say was that he was concerned about her mental health and wanted her to be happy. He apologized for his outburst and stated that he was just disappointed in not being able to arrange for a visit.

Marianna sidestepped these overtures by telling him that she wanted to meet with him. He was taken by surprise. She was now in control. She told him that she had many questions for him and she hoped he could answer them candidly. In typical fashion, Tony wanted to have the conversation there and then, either by phone or on Skype, but Marianna stuck to her guns. She told him that she was willing to meet him halfway up the coast.

Since he lived in the San Francisco area, they could meet someplace near Morro Bay, which was a four-hour drive for both of them; approximately half the distance from Los Angeles to San Francisco. Tony hesitated at first, but then conceded. They decided they would meet on the following Saturday, figuring that they could each leave their respective cities at around eight in the morning and be at Morro Bay roughly by noon. That would give them several hours together before they would have to leave for the return trip.

Marianna smiled when she hung up, feeling empowered. She wanted to see his face when she told him what she had learned. She wanted to watch his body language, thinking that it would be more difficult for him to lie to her face.

CHAPTER SIX

G rant was not happy about Marianna going on this journey at all, but the thought of her going alone was even more unsettling to him. He had been supportive every step of the way as she re-united with her birth father. But now, after hearing about how Tony treated Marianna and learning about his family connections with the Mafia, he was nervous about her safety. Perhaps he had watched too many crime shows. But Mariana was insistent about going – by herself. She believed that this was something she had to do and, though she understood Grant's concerns, she felt that she was perfectly capable of taking care of herself. Grant knew that when Marianna made up her mind to do something, there would be no talking her out of it. She was as stubborn as a mule and as tenacious as a pit bull. The fact that she was a third-degree black belt in karate helped him rationalize that she would be okay. But still, he felt uncomfortable about her being alone with Tony. He wished he could go with her.

Saturday morning arrived. The sky was clear, with temperatures in the 70s. The surf along Highway 1, locally known as PCH, or the Pacific Coast Highway, was rolling with one to two-foot swells. It was a perfect day for taking a drive along the coast to Morro Bay. But Marianna hardly noticed. She was completely absorbed with thoughts about meeting Tony. She hadn't seen him in the flesh since they'd met for the first time on the set of Reality Productions. She couldn't help thinking about what she might learn from Tony about his family. She wondered whether there were members of his family still connected with the Mafia. Or whether he was still involved. She also thought about Dawn and Jane and whether they knew about Tony's family and his involvement with the organization. It was difficult to imagine that they didn't; although when she thought about the secrets in her own family, it was quite possible that they knew nothing of his past. She already had experienced his ability to lie. The thoughts kept on coming, just like the waves. But after a while, they became repetitive. She shook her head, trying to clear them away.

She turned the satellite radio to a blues station. Looking out the window, she realized that she had passed through Carpentaria and was just entering Santa Barbara. She had driven for about ninety minutes, oblivious to everything going on around her. Traffic was light, heading north. A couple of convertibles passed her on the left as she passed a truck on her right on the three-lane freeway. A lone motorcycle cruised in the distance.

It was slightly after noon when Marianna reached Morro Bay. Marianna and Tony had agreed to meet at a very popular public restaurant on the pier near the rock at Morro Bay. Pulling into the parking lot at the entrance to the pier, she glanced toward the big rock rising out of the sea. The sky was clear blue, and she breathed in the ocean air as if fortifying herself for the ordeal ahead. Morro Bay skies were without the yellow haze of smog that she was accustomed to seeing in LA. *Given the state of things,* she wondered, *how long will it be before those blue skies are affected by carbon emissions?* She knew the redwoods in the area were already being damaged by climate change. *Much like the climate of my perfect life, soon to be changed – but I hope not irreparably damaged.*

Marianna felt her pulse quicken as she approached the iconic Dockside Restaurant overlooking the pier with the famous Morro Bay rock in the distance. Fishermen lined both sides of the pier's walkway, their lines dangling into the water. The restaurant was typical beach style, with rough-hewn wood tables and a nautical motif. She spotted Tony, who was seated in a booth overlooking the water.

As she approached the table, Tony stood when he spotted her moving toward him, arms outstretched, ready to give her a hug. Marianna backed away, clearly sending the message that she was not feeling particularly close to him. Tony dropped his arms and sat back down as Marianna slid into the booth across from him without removing her black knee-length coat. She just sat and looked at Tony without saying a word.

Tony's eyes searched Marianna's face for a clue as to how to proceed. She revealed nothing. She just stared at him, her face impassive. Finally, he began talking.

"Look, Marianna, I'm sorry. I didn't mean to go off on you. I was – am - so excited about having you in my life, I just wanted to see you and get to know you." He looked at her with raised brows, his eyes searching her face, beseeching her for understanding. "The thought of losing you again is devastating. I never had biological children of my own. I always wanted them. But after marrying Dawn I found out that I was not able to have kids. When you turned up in my life, I was ecstatic. When you indicated that you were not ready to meet Dawn and Jane, it seemed that you were backing off, backing out of my life. I panicked. I was scared.

And, well, maybe when I am scared, I lash out. I guess I did - lash out, that is."

Marianna didn't know whether to believe him. She'd expected more defensiveness from Tony, figuring he would try to justify his behavior. But that didn't happen, leaving her uncertain as to how to proceed. While in other areas of her life she could be somewhat impulsive, when it came to relationships she was quite cautious and preferred to move slowly, trusting her feelings to guide her.

Her stomach and shoulders relaxed. There were more issues to discuss. She hoped the conversation would continue to be as amicable. Marianna sat quietly, looking at Tony, before replying. "I appreciate your apology, Tony. It's just that I don't want to rush into a full blown, already-existing family before I have totally resolved matters in my own family. My parents are just getting used to the idea that I know you exist, let alone that I've met you."

"That makes sense," replied Tony. "I have gone forty-nine years without having a biological child. I guess I can wait a little longer." He chuckled.

"What about your own family?" asked Marianna. "Your wife and daughter must have some of the same reservations I have. After all; suddenly here comes a twenty-eight-year-old interloper arriving on the scene. It's gonna take some digesting before they come to terms with the idea that you have another child. I mean, Jane has been an only child for her entire life."

"You're right, of course," said Tony with a grin. "Where did you get such wisdom?"

Marianna felt her face grow warm. "I don't know about wisdom; it's just common sense."

She decided that this would be a good time to tell Tony what she had learned from her parents. "How much did you know about my mother's pregnancy?"

Tony's mood became sober. "Like I've told you before, I didn't know anything about your mother being pregnant. Until the show, I didn't know you even existed."

Marianna fixed Tony with steely eyes, feeling her stomach tighten. She suddenly felt detached. She turned cold and spoke deliberately. "My mother told me that she met you when she was seventeen and you were finishing your senior year at college. You were visiting the west coast during winter break. She had a crush on you. You dated her. One evening invited her out on a date that ended up back at a friend's apartment while he was out of town. Once there, you seduced her and the two of you had sex." *J'accuse* she thought.

The color drained from Tony's face. His eyes averted hers. He swallowed.

She leaned across the table. "She was seventeen and you were twenty-one. That's rape!"

Tony began nodding his head as he realized who Marianna's mother was. His eyes filled with tears.

Marianna continued in the same detached manner. "And then your father, Louie Donatello, a well-known Mafia mobster, had his goons pay my mother and father a visit. At first, they threatened to take me away from them. He tried to buy them off, but they wouldn't be bought. So instead, he threatened to hurt me and them if they ever told anyone. My parents kept their word all these years – until now, when they told me the entire story."

By this time, tears were rolling down Tony's cheeks. "I didn't know that was you. Until this moment I didn't know who your mother was. I was a wild twenty-one-year-old kid. I fooled around with a lot of girls back then. When you told me about your mother, I pictured someone else."

"But now you remember?" asked Marianna.

Tony nodded. "Yeah, now I remember."

"That's bullshit, Tony!" exclaimed Marianna. "Unless you have a slew of babies out there somewhere. How many times have you been confronted by a pregnant teen who wants to marry you? That doesn't happen every day!"

Marianna glared at him, her fists clenched.

"And you took advantage of my mother." She spat out the words.

Tony slowly nodded, his guilt mounting. "I haven't thought about her in more than twenty-five years. I remember it all. I remember your mother. I remember her telling me she was pregnant. I reacted horribly. And I was more than willing to sign the papers giving up my parental rights. I was a kid. I'm sorry. Very sorry." He paused, taking a handkerchief out of his pocket to wipe his eyes. "But I didn't know anything about my father's threat or the deal he struck with your parents. This is the first I am hearing about it. You've got to believe me," he implored.

"Is this part of your dark past that you alluded to during our previous conversations and texts?" asked Marianna.

Tony's face clouded over. He remained silent. Slowly he again began nodding his head.

"When I was a youth, and through most of my twenties, I was pretty wild," began Tony. "I was being groomed to take my place in *la cosa nostra*. My father is Louie Donatello, a crime boss on the East Coast. Because of the power wielded by my father, I was able to get away with a lot of stuff; a lot of it bad. I sowed more than a few wild oats. And, unfortunately, your mother was included in that period of my life when I was irresponsible. But I swear to you that I did not know of any deal that was struck between my father and your parents. I didn't know until now that he even knew of your existence. I haven't a clue how he found out." Tony paused for a moment. "And I regret not having stood up like a man when your mother told me she was pregnant."

Tony sounded contrite. Marianna wanted to believe him. They both accepted that he had lied to her about not knowing her mother was pregnant. Even if he did not know until now that the girl who, twenty-eight years ago, told him she was pregnant, and who later had asked him to sign papers permitting an adoption, was her mother, he knew that he had impregnated someone and had done nothing all of these years to find out who it was. Some little girl was destined to grow up without knowing her *bio-dad*. Marianna just happened to be that little girl.

Marianna took her time asking her next question. She slowed her breathing and relaxed her stomach. "Did you – did you ever think of trying to find out about the child my mother was carrying – your child? You admit that you knew you had impregnated my mother. Did you ever try to find … me?"

Tony held her eyes with his. He slowly shook his head. "No. I thought of it from time, but never actually looked. I didn't want to, uh, what was the word you used before? Interloper. I didn't want to be an interloper. I didn't want to intrude on your life or the life of your family. I thought it would be better to let it go."

Marianna was pleased to hear that he at least thought of her. She accepted his explanation and decided not to pursue the issue further. She wanted to press forward with her agenda. She wanted to know more about her grandfather and Tony's East Coast family. She wasn't sure how to approach the subject, so she just plunged right in.

"Is your father still alive?" she asked. "Is Louie Donatello alive?"

"Yes," replied Tony. He looked off into the distance as he spoke. "He is over eighty years old and I suspect he's as feisty as ever. He lives in New York near my brother and two sisters, who keep an eye on him."

"Do you have much contact with him?" asked Marianna.

"No. I haven't spoken to him in over twenty years." His voice was calm, matter of fact. His face remained stoic.

"And your brother and sisters - do you have contact with them?" Marianna was curious about the back story, but knew she had to proceed with caution.

Tony turned his head toward her. "I rarely speak to them. I wouldn't say we were close. We have little in common."

"What happened? I mean, why don't you have contact with them?" asked Marianna.

"Let's say I didn't leave New York under the friendliest of terms with my father, and my siblings sided with him," replied Tony speaking in the same matter-of-fact tone.

"Do you mind my asking what happened? Why did you leave?" inquired Marianna.

"It's a long story," began Tony. His eyes glazed over as he spoke. He stared out the window focusing on the huge rock in the middle of the bay. It was not a story he liked remembering much less telling. Marianna waited.

"I was born the son of a Mafia captain. In that world, being a capo's son is a pretty big deal. As the firstborn son, I was expected to take his place someday. Like any large organization, I was expected to start at the bottom and work my way up. But, of course, as the son of the boss, I was treated differently. I accelerated up the corporate ladder faster than the average person. The job came with some perks and some liabilities. On the plus side, I moved up faster, made more money, and always had someone watching my back. I could get away with things that others couldn't."

Like knocking up young girls and walking away without paying a price, thought Marianna.

Tony continued. "On the downside, I was always under surveillance. Everything I did was reported back to my old man. And there was a code of behavior I was supposed to honor. I was expected to be better than others. The bar was higher for me. The chain of command is similar to what you see in any other large corporation. The only thing significantly different are the products and services we offer. And, of course, the ethics and morals are different for the Mafia than for General Electric.

"So I started out as an enforcer in the loan sharking part of the business. My job was to make sure that people paid their debts and paid them on time. If they didn't, me and my crew had to go out and collect, often using force. Early on, I realized that I didn't have the stomach to do the things that were required of me. I couldn't physically hurt people on command; especially the desperate people who were forced to go to a loan shark for money to pay the rent. And then came a day of reckoning," continued Tony. "I was supposed to earn my stripes. I was supposed to become a made-man."

"Made-man? What's that mean?" asked Marianna.

Tony looked at her, his eyes penetrating hers. "I was supposed to kill someone. A contract killing."

Marianna gulped. Her eyes widened. She swallowed hard. "And did you?"

Tony slowly shook his head. "No. I couldn't do it. So, I asked my father and grandfather to let me go; to permit me to leave the organization. At first they refused, arguing that no one leaves *la famiglia*. But they knew I would leave anyway, and then they would have to put a contract out on me. I guess they didn't want to go that far. So, they relented. I wanted to get as far away from the mob as I could. I moved to California and got into construction. It was something I knew about. After a few years, I met and married Dawn. Her daughter Jane was two years old at the time."

Marianna sat open-mouthed. She imagined the *Sopranos*. She knew that Tony Soprano broke bones. She thought of all the mobster movies she had watched. She never thought about the steps necessary to become a wiseguy. And she certainly never considered the mafia as like other large, international corporations. She felt weird sitting across the table from someone who actually was in that business. It felt even weirder to think that this man was her *bio-dad*.

Marianna wasn't sure she completely believed Tony; particularly about his not knowing about the deal his father had struck with her parents. She scratched her head and fiddled with her ponytail. His story sounded a lot like other stories she had heard from men whose fathers were very controlling and expected their sons to take over the family business, who would disinherit their sons if they didn't follow through with their plan. Her gut told her that there was more to the story than Tony was telling her.

She braced herself for the next subject she was about to bring up and again just pushed forward. "I want to meet my grandfather," she blurted, her tone strident.

Tony glared at her in disbelief. Now it was his turn to sit with his eyes widened. "You're kidding, right? Why in the world would you want to meet him?" asked Tony, his voice moving up a notch.

She wasn't about to acknowledge that she was still trying to understand her own motivation. She sat quietly for a moment.

"He *is* my grandfather, isn't he?" Marianna pressed on. "And if I'm going to be part of your life, I want to meet the rest of *my* family. I want to meet your brother and sisters and their families as well." Marianna could feel her heart quicken as she anticipated Tony's response. She could see that he was getting agitated.

"I told you that I haven't seen my father in over twenty years," said Tony through clenched his teeth. "You don't know him. And you don't know the kind of people they are. This is *la cosa nostra,* for Christ's sake!" His eyes turned to steel. His teeth clenched.

Marianna persisted. "If I am going to be part of your family in California, I want to know about your family in New York," she exclaimed, her jaw jutting out. "I want to make my own decisions about who they are – and what they do." She had to admit to herself that the thought of having a mafia honcho as a grandfather and relatives who were in the mob heightened her sense of adventure and drove her forward.

"Are your sisters and brother in the business?" asked Marianna.

"Oh yes, my sisters, their husbands and their children, along with my brother, his wife, and their kids; they're all involved in one way or another," replied Tony. "Like I said, it's a family business – except for me. I'm the pariah. And that's why we have little contact."

"So let me get this straight, Tony," began Marianna, trying to speak softly and concisely. "You are the son of a Mafia boss. You started in the business, couldn't stomach its violence and criminal aspect, and decided to get out. You started a new life in California, became a contractor, got married, and adopted a little girl. When you were a young man, you learned that my mother was pregnant, kissed it off, and twenty-eight years later discovered that she had a daughter – me – and now you want me to be part of your life. But not your whole life; just a part of it. Have I got that right?"

Tony stared at her. "Well, yeah, you got it right. Except that the reason I don't want you part of that life is because I am trying to protect you; don't you get that?" entreated Tony.

In sudden pique of frustration, Tony reached out and grabbed Marianna's arm.

"You're being stupid! You don't know what you're asking for!" he hissed.

Marianna stared at him, looked down at his hand on her arm, and then back at him. Tony removed his hand from her apologetically. He tried to explain to her that getting involved with that side of his family would not be a good idea on multiple levels, telling her that she would be getting more than she bargained for and would be opening a can of worms that'd best be left unopened.

But Marianna dug in her heals. "He already knows of my existence. He made a deal with my parents. For all you know he might have been keeping an eye on me for the past twenty-eight years!" She looked around the restaurant. "Maybe someone is watching me – us – right now."

Tony glanced around and smiled. "You've got quite an imagination, Marianna."

She pressed Tony to make an introduction to his father, the eighty-something-year-old Louie Donatello. Finally, Tony relented. He told Marianna that he would connect her with one of her cousins in New York where Louie lived. He might be willing to arrange to take Marianna to meet his father. Tony made it clear to Marianna that he did not want to talk to or see his father and would not reach out to him in any way. She would have to go it alone.

CHAPTER SEVEN

On the drive back home, Marianna went over every moment of her meeting with Tony, including his grabbing her arm. That was the second time she'd seen an aggressive side to him. She mused over the fact that in both instances he was able to recognize his mistake, and had apologized. *Perhaps it wasn't a need to control,* she wondered, *but rather, a protective instinct. Maybe I was wrong about him. Maybe he changed from the boy he was to the man he has become.*

She wanted to believe his story about not knowing about the deal that had been struck between his father and her parents. She also knew that many young men had fathered children they knew nothing about. Girls sometimes got pregnant and didn't tell the baby's father, or didn't even know who was the father of their child. And many young men didn't know or didn't care that they were fathers. Her own parents weren't interested in knowing more about Marianna's birth father. They had created a life together. Life was good. But now things were different. Marianna was on a mission to know her origins. She knew she would be upsetting everyone. Meeting Tony had changed everything. But that toothpaste couldn't be put back into the tube. She felt a mixture of excitement and trepidation as she anticipated the next phase of her journey.

The sun was setting along the California coast. Driving south the ocean was now on her right. The sight itself relaxed her. She was glad she had made the drive to meet Tony and now had the time to reflect upon the meeting. The traffic was moderate; it was Saturday night. She was in no hurry so she stayed in the right-hand lane embracing the time alone. Cars zipped past her and she gave wide birth to the motorcycle that wove between the lanes and passed her as well. *Gotta share the road,* she thought.

She continued to wonder why she was becoming obsessed with knowing about Tony and the rest of his family. She tried to rationalize that it was important, even if for no other reason than wanting to know her own medical history and genetic predispositions. But she knew herself better than that. She had an insatiable curiosity about life in general, but this was different. This was digging into her own roots. She knew that she couldn't just let it go. She had to admit that the idea that she might be part of a Mafia family captivated her and, if she was honest with herself, titillated her. She thought about what she had said to Tony about the possibility of being watched by the mafia all these years. It gave her a chill, but she smiled nevertheless. *Wouldn't that be something,* she thought. *All these years my capo grandfather might have been having me watched.*

Marianna had always been fearless, even going back to middle school. She was afraid of nothing and no one. The boys thought she was hot, but they quickly learned not to mess around with her. The girls found her intimidating. She was not a typical girly-girl. Her first major confrontation with school authorities came over the issue of separating the boys from the girls in competitive sports. Marianna felt that she was as good as most of the boys in her school and she wanted to compete against them. This was especially true when it came to both track and swimming. She easily was faster than all the girls in school, and most of the boys. She wanted a chance to complete against the best. The school and most of the parents were against co-ed competitions, leaving Marianna infuriated. But she was not deterred. She would find another way to compete.

After school hours she took up martial arts, where there was no distinction made between boys and girls. By the time she graduated high school she had earned a black belt in Shaolin Kempo, a martial art that combined karate and kung fu. She also became a competitive gymnast, earning a varsity letter. In college, she studied kickboxing, in which she earned a second black belt. The Japanese dojos, where she trained off-campus, were all co-ed. Competitions were based on skill level and rank, not on gender or even size or weight. Black belts competed against black belts. Marianna took on all comers, winning the majority of her matches. She had a collection of medals and trophies that lined her dormitory shelves. Between the martial arts and gymnastics, Marianna felt confident in her ability to handle herself in a physical altercation.

Her feisty attitude was not limited to athletics. She developed an assertive personality and fought for the rights of underdogs, becoming a feminist and an animal rights advocate. Whether the case involved a human or an animal, she would always fight for the disenfranchised and disempowered.

She also had a dark side, holding an affinity for the marginalized, the outcasts, and people who lived on the streets. She felt far more comfortable with them than the folks who lived in the upscale neighborhoods. She saw the street people as more real, without pretense, more authentic.

As a child living in suburban Oregon, she'd often thought of becoming an undercover cop. She saw this as an opportunity to help the addicts and prostitutes who were easy prey for the predators who used them. As a teen and later as a young adult she volunteered to work in inner city schools and Boys and Girls Clubs working with under-privileged children. She learned about the hardships they faced and she wanted to do something about it.

But she also found the street life intriguing – even appealing. She heard the stories of life on the street, the gangs, living on the other side of the law. She understood gang members and their desire to feel a sense of power when they could manipulate the system and get away with breaking the law. Unlike other law enforcement wannabes, Marianna did not judge the gangbangers.

She also continued to dream of being an undercover cop, figuring she could be in both worlds at the same time. On the one hand, she could be hanging out on the streets living with the people who inhabited the underworld, while on the other hand, being on the side of the law. She also figured that her martial arts and gymnastics skills would make her a perfect candidate for the police academy. When she entered college, she majored in criminology after finding out that it would give her advanced standing in the academy.

But this dream went up in smoke when, at twenty years old, while still in college, she was diagnosed with uterine cancer. She'd spent the next year in and out of the hospital, underwent both chemo and radiation treatments, lost her hair, and missed a year of college. The surgery required removal of both of her ovaries. She would never be able to have children.

She began going through the various stages of grief beginning with anger. She was angry about losing her ovaries and never being able to have children. She was angry that she lost her passion for gymnastics. She was angry at God. She began to act out her anger by picking fights with people. First they were verbal fights – she became downright surly. Anyone could piss her off. Then she turned to looking for physical fights. She went into the inner-city's most dangerous areas cruising for trouble. But this didn't last long. One night, she picked a fight with the wrong dude in a rave club and almost got killed. If it wasn't for a quirk of fate – an off-duty cop stepping in front of the big guy about to take her out – she would have been back in the hospital only this time with broken bones, or worse, rather than cancer.

She hooked up with a wild crowd that was more of a gang than just a clique. Despite her typical middleclass upbringing, Marianna craved excitement: not just the typical excitement of a rave club, drugs or alcohol, but something more dangerous. She needed the distraction and she needed to feel alive. She and her friends hooked up with some inner-city kids who connected her to some people who had a methamphetamine lab in the basement. Marianna convinced them that they could score bigger if they sold in the white middleclass neighborhoods where she and her friends lived. She and her crew became the uptown crack dealers in her suburban high school. Everything was going well for a few months until the meth lab exploded, killing the kid who ran it.

But that didn't stop Marianna from coming up with another scheme to satisfy her need for excitement. She fostered the idea of burglarizing homes in the upscale neighborhoods near where she lived. She and her crew knew many of the kids who lived there and knew when these families would be on vacation or away for the weekend. She also knew that most of the people who lived in two-story homes did not have burglar alarms on the second floor.

Armed with this knowledge, she began her foray into the world of breaking and entering. She became a cat burglar of sorts. And she loved the thought of it. It was short lived, however. She hadn't counted on a dog being left in one house; nor a video camera recording her climbing through the second story bedroom window. She didn't figure on the homeowners having installed a security service with video monitoring. The security company witnessed Marianna climbing through the window and called the police, who arrived just as she was climbing down the ladder. Fortunately for her, the homeowners did not press charges. They knew Marianna's parents; she was let off with a warning. Being middle class and white was a definite perk.

These two experiences were enough to make her realize that she had much to learn if she was going to live on the wrong side of the law. As her anger subsided she was able to think more clearly. *It's funny,* she thought, *how strong emotions and a confrontation with death can override any sense of morality; it's also much easier to go straight than go down the criminal path.*

Her bout with cancer, and the realization that she could be susceptible to a recurrence, left her feeling vulnerable – she hated the feeling. With the encouragement of the people in the cancer support group to which her oncologist referred her, Marianna sought out the help of Dr. Harold Sherman, a psychotherapist who specialized in the treatment of cancer survivors.

Dr. Sherman was a deeply compassionate and spiritual man who understood the challenges cancer victims faced in coming to terms with a disease for which there was often no cure, only remission. It was like having an uninvited guest living in the shadows of your body ready to make an appearance at any time. He knew that it didn't matter how low the probability of a recurrence, cancer survivors worried. He understood how difficult it was for people to accept being out of control and vulnerable, especially those who prided themselves on being independent. He recognized that Marianna was definitely one of those.

He encouraged Marianna to embrace all of her feelings: her anger, her fear, her weakness as well as her love, her power, and her strength.

"Human beings, Marianna, are a composite of opposites or dualities," he explained. "And gradations in between. We all have built-in contradictions. It is the struggle between these polarities that helps define us. Cancer victims have a very real sense of mortality. It is not just knowing intellectually that we are all going to die, but in a very real way you have come face to face with death. The big question is, how will you come to terms with your mortality? Will you fall into despair or will you embrace that reality and move forward to create the life you want despite knowing that it could all come to an abrupt end?"

Marianna sat quietly taking in Dr. Sherman's words.

"I'm sure as shit not going to give up," she replied defiantly. "I'm going to kick this cancer's ass!"

Dr. Sherman smiled. He loved her spunk. He knew that it was a fine line between being a cancer survivor and a cancer victim. Marianna was a survivor. He introduced her to the Jungian analyst's concept of the shadow, the unconscious dark side in all human beings, that contains parts of our personality that are not acceptable to the conscious mind.

"We were able to see your dark side come out when you were diagnosed with cancer," Dr Sherman explained. "You became so angry that you didn't think about the morality of your behavior; you didn't even think about the potential consequences. You just acted."

"You're right," she replied. "I was so pissed, I couldn't think straight! I just wanted to do something to prove I was alive. I wanted to fight. The adrenalin rush camouflaged the fear and covered the weakness I felt."

"Your shadow took over," reflected Dr. Sherman.

Marianna continued to work with Dr. Sherman until she graduated from college. She explored all aspects of her life with him; she trusted him and felt safe. They explored her future plans, her family life, and her relationships. Dr. Sherman probed her about having only recently learned that her father was not her birth father. He wondered whether she was curious about finding him. Marianna told him that she had tentatively tried to find him but came up empty-handed. Dr. Sherman knew better than to push it thinking, *when she's ready she'll be ready, not before.*

Rather than acting out further, she spent her leisure time reading crime thriller novels and watching television series and movies where the lead characters all had a dark and a light side. On the surface, they appeared to be law-abiding citizens, but beneath their public persona lurked another, darker, and sometimes sinister side. *Their shadow,* thought Marianna. She also enjoyed the reverse scenario, where the protagonist was mostly dark, but had a soft spot. She could identify with them. As an actress, she was drawn to these roles. She identified with strong women who could make it in typically male-dominated careers – a detective who killed perpetrators who had gotten away with murder, a defense attorney who worked for organized crime, or a physician who did not honor the Hippocratic Oath – do no harm – when it came to rapists. These were her heroes. They were the outliers.

Instead of acting out or becoming depressed, Marianna took a different direction. She decided to learn everything she could about cancer. She took on cancer as she would any opponent, and was determined to beat it. The pit-bull in her took over. She directed her anger toward the big C. She learned about food production and its relationship to cancer. She discovered that the pesticides used in farming, chemical additives, and genetic modification all were linked to the development of cancer. Marianna always took care of her body. Now she was more determined than ever to make her body healthy enough to resist cancer. She thought that, just as it was possible to develop weed and insect resistant soil in which vegetables grew without using chemicals, it may also be possible to develop an immune system that would be resistant to cancer.

She knew it was impossible to guarantee that she would never develop cancer again, but she could make it more difficult for the cancer cells to grow and metastasize. The biggest change she made was to give up eating any animal products, including meat, fish, and dairy. She learned that most animals were fed with products that contained pesticides. Even grasses were loaded with pesticides. Many animals that humans consumed were genetically modified. Fish swam in waters containing mercury and other pollutants. She understood that, if she ate them, the pollutants would enter her body. Hence, Marianna became a vegan, eating only plant-based products.

Marianna's life was a continuous dialectic between the light and the dark, good and evil, sides of her personality. At this stage, she was moving toward the good.

When she returned to college as a junior, she switched majors from criminology to nutrition and physical therapy. She double-majored in kinesthesiology and nutrition, which led her obtaining certificates as both a physical therapist and dietitian in addition to her college degree. Her vegan lifestyle also fostered her interest as an animal rights activist. Now it became a political issue, both in terms of the rights of animals and in terms of fighting for organic farming and feed for livestock. Animals became her new form of fighting for the underdog – literally. Animals became her children; she would have adopted all stray animals if she could.

During her recovery from cancer, Marianna met a woman in her cancer survivor's group who was an actress. They became close friends. The woman was the catalyst for Marianna to study acting. She introduced her to an agent, who found a bit part for Marianna in a television show where she had to play the part of a recovering addict. Marianna loved the experience so much that she began taking acting classes as a side gig to her work as a physical trainer and nutritionist.

By the time she auditioned for the Reality Productions television show where she met Tony, she had developed a thriving practice as a physical trainer with a special affinity for cancer survivors, and had acted in several TV shows and a couple of movies.

With this history, the idea of meeting her biological father's mafia family didn't frighten her. Quite the contrary; she was excited about it. She had survived cancer, confronted bullies, earned black belts, and faced tough auditions and audiences. *How difficult could it be to meet an eighty-year-old man and his family?* she thought.

All the way home, Marianna kept thinking about meeting her grandfather, cousins, and other family members in New York. She wondered how she was going to explain all of this to Grant. She knew that she would have to spend some time on the East Coast, and that wouldn't please him; especially since she intended to go without him. Grant was very protective of her, and the idea of her being on her own with this underworld family wouldn't go over well with him.

As she drove into the driveway of their home, she saw Grant tinkering with his favorite toy – his motorcycle. Marianna paused for a moment remembering the motorcycles she had noticed while she was on the road. *Could he have followed me?* she wondered. *I know he's protective, but… or am I just being paranoid because of thoughts about Louie watching me?* She shook her head trying to clear her mind. *Focus, girl!* She smiled at Grant, parked her car, and walked into the house. Grant put his arm around her and walked along with her. Marianna made them both a cup of tea.

When she told Grant about her visit with Tony and what she had learned about her grandfather, Louie Donatello, Grant just sat there staring at her as she unfolded the events of the day. But when she told him that she wanted to spend a week or more in New York getting to know that side of her biological family, he stared at her in disbelief.

"Seriously! Are you friggin' kidding me?" exclaimed Grant. He looked at her with a dumbfounded expression on his face, his hands spread for emphasis.

Marianna expected he would not be pleased with her decision. She could feel the blood rushing to her face. She dug in her heels, ready for battle. "Yeah, I'm serious. I've got an entire family back there that I have never met. It's important to me to at least get to know them. And it is important that they meet me. I don't want to be invisible. And I realized that I want to be part of a larger family. I am an only child. It might be nice to have cousins near my age."

Grant hesitated for a moment as he considered what he wanted to say. He knew how obstinate Marianna could be. "I get the part about wanting a larger family. It's WHO the other part is that concerns me. Sometimes being invisible might be a good thing, babe," said Grant, speaking softly. "Especially when it comes to dealing with potentially dangerous people. Your grandfather already threatened you and your parents once. What makes you think they won't do it again? You could be putting your parents in danger."

Marianna stared at Grant. "I'm no threat to his family. The statute of limitations on statutory rape in Oregon has long past. So, what's the threat? What is it that you're really worried about, Grant?"

Now it was Grant's turn to think. He knew she was right; she didn't pose any substantial threat. "Maybe," he began as he looked at the floor, "I am worried that, if you visit them, you might not want to come back from the exciting life of the granddaughter of a crime boss living in the Big Apple." When he looked up, Marianna saw that his eyes were wet.

She smiled. "Hey, hon, I'm not about to leave the life we created together. And I am certainly not going to leave you. This is just something I've got to do." She got up from where she was seated and walked behind him, placing her arms around him. She pressed her head against his.

Grant looked up at her. "I'll miss you while you're gone and still wish you wouldn't go, but I know you. Once you make up your mind to do something, nothing can stop you. I hope you have thought of your parents. I can't imagine they're going to be too thrilled that you want to meet the guy who threatened them. It must be hard enough on them to know that you are in contact with the man who abandoned your mother when he learned she was pregnant. And it's got to be tough on your dad to know that you met your birth father. Now you're going to meet the rest of this new family. That's gonna be tough on the family you already have."

Marianna felt a pang. "Maybe I didn't think enough about how they might react," she murmured. "But when do I just get to think about me for a change? If I think too much about them – or you – I won't do anything!"

"I understand, but I can't help wonder what other things you might not have considered," replied Grant. "In your zeal to move forward, you might leave a lot of damage in your wake."

This led to several more hours of conversation, sometimes quite heated, as Marianna blocked and countered Grant's every objection as though she was sparring in the dojo. Her mind was made up. She knew that she had to talk with her parents, and that wouldn't be easy. *But this is my life*, she thought, *and I am going to do what I need to do – even if some people may be upset with me. Who knows how much time I have left on this planet?*

Grant was quite right. Her parents were none too pleased with her decision to contact her birth father's family. Everyone in her family was against her decision. They were scared for her and for themselves. But Marianna had made up her mind. For most of her adult life, Marianna had put the needs and wishes of others before her own. Not this time. The more they argued, the more steadfast she became and the more impatient she was to hear from Tony about the contact in New York.

Marianna knew that the journey she was about to embark upon would change her life forever. But she also knew that it was something she had to do. Meeting her biological father had raised more questions than it had answered, questions that she never could have anticipated. And the answers to those questions would fill in the pieces of the puzzle that formed her life. Such is the plight of a curious person. When she delved into something - anything - she left no stone unturned. She became like the forensic criminologist walking the grid.

Several days later, she received an email from Tony indicating that he had obtained contact information for Angelo, his brother Mike's son. Tony told Marianna that Angelo, who was almost the same age as Marianna, was willing to meet her at the airport in New York and introduce her to members of the family. Tony said Angelo told him that no one in the family was ready to talk to her grandfather about Marianna's visit until after she was in New York and they met her. He explained that no one got an audience with Louie

Donatello until they went through the appropriate vetting process, family or not.

Tony gave Marianna Angelo's contact information and said the rest was up to her; he was not going any further. He also made a final pitch to discourage her, but his warnings fell on deaf ears. Marianna was resolute.

She immediately sent an email to Angelo explaining to him who she was and expressing her interest in meeting her birth father's family - especially her grandfather. This began a spate of emails between the two of them resulting in their setting a date for her visit. She told him that she planned to spend a week or more in New York to give herself time to get to know people, and for them to get to know her. She explained that she was mostly interested in learning about her biological heritage and her genes on her father's side. Angelo seemed friendly enough and indicated that he was looking forward to meeting her. They set the date. Angelo planned on picking her up at JFK on May 1st, about three weeks away. They exchanged photos so they would recognize one another at the airport.

CHAPTER EIGHT

A few days after she returned from seeing Tony, Marianna received a call from Joseph Pendergast, the Reality Productions producer, who told her that the show was going to air within the next several weeks or so. They were putting together promotional pieces comprised of clips from the actual show; teasers that would start airing within the next few days. He explained that they had to start early to create some buzz about the new series and were planning to use her segment as part of the series promo. Pendergast wanted Marianna to be available for interviews. He was hoping the news media would be interested in talking with her, especially since her segment of the show was going to air first. Not knowing exactly how long she would be in New York, Marianna told Pendergast that she would be unavailable for the month of May. Not to be put off, Pendergast told her that she could do some promotional work out of their New York offices. It was important that she make herself available, if necessary.

Two weeks later Marianna received a call from her mother, who was frantic.

"Hi, Mom, what's up?" asked Marianna.

"Marianna, Dad and I just saw one of the clips from the upcoming show," began Mary. "Neither of us realized that this was going to be released nationally. We thought it was going to be a low budget, local show."

"No, it's a cable network show that might even go international," replied Marianna, mistaking her mother's frantic tone for excitement. "Wouldn't that be great?"

"Not really, dear," said Mary, her voice trembling. "Actually, it worries us. What will happen when Tony's family in New York sees it? They'll know where you are."

Marianna hesitated before replying. She knew it was time to tell her mother that she was planning to visit Tony's family in New York.

"Mom, they probably already know where I am and where you are," replied Marianna. "Tony contacted one of his nephews, Angelo."

"How do you know that?" Mary asked. Her voice quivered revealing signs of panic.

"Tony told me," replied Marianna. She cautiously tried to feel her mother out. "I am going to meet Angelo and the family in New York." Marianna knew it was not going to go over well.

"What? When?" exclaimed Mary. She held the phone with both hands.

"On May 1st. I will be going to New York for a week or two to meet them." She paused for a moment before continuing. "I know it's upsetting to you and to Dad, but it's something I feel I must do. I want to put the puzzle pieces together to have a complete picture of who I am and where I come from."

Mary fretted. "It worries me, sweetheart. You don't know these people. It could be dangerous."

Marianna heard her mother's concern, but had a fleeting feeling of irritation. "I don't think so, Mom," replied Marianna. "And besides, I am a big girl. I can take care of myself." *Marianna do it 'self.* It offended her that her mother continued to see her as incapable of taking care of herself. She would have preferred her mother to be more empathetic about her desire to meet her other family and, if she had to say anything, to simply advise, "Be careful." Even now, Marianna could not entertain the notion that her mother might be concerned for her own and her father's safety.

On the day of her departure, Grant drove her to LAX. He had come to accept that there was nothing he could do to change Marianna's mind. After years of marriage, he knew that once she was set on something, there was no changing course. Marianna promised him that she would leave at the first sign of trouble and would keep in daily contact with him either by text or Skype. Grant dropped her off at American Airlines; but his eyes followed her through the terminal doors until she disappeared into the crowd. He pulled away from the curb, thinking, *I hope you find what you're looking for. And come home safely.*

Grant was totally accepting of Marianna. He knew her strengths and her vulnerabilities. He knew she struggled with her demons, especially the Big-C – the uninvited guest, as they referred to her cancer. He knew also that he was not Mr. Excitement. So, he gave her lots of room to experiment with adventure. Just as he was not a dancer, he was not a risk-taker. She was both. And he did not want to squelch either by trying to impose his style on her. So, he often stood in the wings, watching.

Marianna went through security checks without any problems and her plane was on time. If all went well, she would arrive at JFK at about 6 PM Eastern time. She tried to sleep on the plane to make the time go more quickly, but found it difficult. She was far too excited about what was soon to unfold in New York.

She had arranged for Angelo to meet her by the baggage claim section of the terminal. She recognized him immediately. He was about six feet tall with dark, curly hair that hung to his shoulders. He had her olive complexion and green eyes. They could have been siblings. Angelo smiled on seeing her; a broad, friendly smile with perfect white teeth accompanying a twinkle in his eyes. He immediately embraced her as one would a long lost relative; with total acceptance. Once they collected her luggage, Angelo led her outside the terminal where a Cadillac Escalade with tinted windows was parked illegally, waiting. Standing next to the car was a heavyset, short young man in his twenties, also with curly black hair and dark, deep-set eyes. He smiled when he saw her. His name was Sonny, and he was another cousin who had come to meet her. He was Tony's sister Anne-Marie's son. He gave her a big bear hug. Marianna was startled. *A touchy-feely family.* The thought made her smile.

"Welcome to the Big Apple, cuz," said Sonny with a wide grin as they climbed into the Escalade. "Is this your first time visiting the city?" He tossed her suitcase, roller-board, and backpack in the rear of the Escalade.

"Yeah. First time," replied Marianna. "I kept promising myself that I would do it, but it never happened."

"Well, we'll make sure you getta good taste of the city that never sleeps," said Angelo. "Our first stop now will be my apartment in the SoHo district, downtown. New York is divided into five boroughs and in each borough there are districts. Manhattan is referred to as 'the City'."

"You're a regular fuckin' tour guide, Angie," wisecracked Sonny, giving Angelo a light punch on the shoulder. Angelo flipped him off.

"LA is spread out; a horizontal city with lots of neighborhoods," said Marianna. "New York is vertical; especially – uh – the City." She smiled.

"There you go," said Sonny. "By da time you leave for LA youse'll be talkin' like a native New Yawka."

The three cousins laughed at Sonny's exaggerated New York accent.

"I've got a two-bedroom apartment," said Angelo, "so you can stay as long as you'd like. No problem. It's only a block from the subway, so you'll be able to get around and see whatever you want."

This, too, took Marianna by surprise. She had fully expected to stay in the mid-town hotel where she had booked a room. "Hey, I don't want to put you out, Angelo," she said. "You don't even know me. And besides, I made a reservation."

"Whatta you talkin' about?" he replied. "You're my cousin. I ain't gonna let you stay in no hotel."

"I'll cancel your reservation," added Sonny in agreement.

Marianna didn't know what to say. Rather than being treated like a stranger, she was being treated like a long lost relative. It both felt good and a little disarming. *A bit too much too soon*, she thought. It was similar to Tony's style of instant familiarity. Not at all like she was brought up. The Boltons were far more reserved.

The drive to Angelo's apartment took about an hour. The sun was setting and the city lights came on, transforming the skyline as they entered Manhattan. Marianna kept craning her neck, looking upward as they took the Manhattan Bridge into lower Manhattan. She was awestruck. The streets were teaming with people rushing here and there. It was nothing like Los Angeles, where people, when they did walk, sauntered. People in New York were scurrying. Horns honked and tires screeched. This was Gotham. Marianna half expected to see the bat sign appear in the sky. The thought made her smile.

"Tomorrow," began Angelo, "we will be driving up to the Bronx to the Morris Park area where you're gonna meet the entire family. Everybody is excited to meet you, so be prepared for a lot of questions and a lot of noise."

"Yeah," added Sonny, "it's pretty much like in that movie *My Big Fat Greek Wedding* except that it's a bunch of Italians. Everybody talks loud and at the same time, especially at the dinner table." He chortled.

It sounded so different than what she was accustomed to, thought Marianna. Dinners with her parents were very quiet. Neither of her parents were big talkers.

"The Greeks and the Italians are alike," added Angelo. "They both talk a lot and love food. So be prepared to eat. My mother, Aunt Anne-Marie, Sonny's mom, and Aunt Lena have been preparing all week."

"Will Grandpa Louie be there?" asked Marianna.

Angelo and Sonny looked at each other.

"What?" asked Marianna. "He's my grandfather, and I've never met him."

"I doubt it," replied Angelo. "He's an old man and seldom comes to these family get-togethers anymore. When he was younger, you couldn't keep him away. He would hold court." Sonny nodded in agreement.

They got off the bridge and began going through the city streets toward Angelo's apartment. They were lucky to find a parking space a couple of blocks from Angelo's building. Parking in the City was at a premium. It was not uncommon for people to park several blocks away from their destination.

In the early part of the 20th century the SoHo district was the heart of the textile industry. Then came gentrification, to the point that now it was a trendy, upscale shopping area and the factories had been transformed to a mixed use of artist lofts and apartments. Angelo had bought a loft and re-modeled it into a large open area with two bedrooms. He decorated it in a high-tech style quite in contrast to the 1900s structure with its ultra-high ceilings and large industrial windows. They entered the loft using a freight elevator that stopped at each floor. Marianna was impressed with Angelo's attention to detail.

"This is very cool," said Marianna as her eyes scanned the space. "You've got a good eye for design, Angelo."

"That's our cuz, cousin," said Sonny with a smirk. "He's a real fashionista."

"You think that way because you're a slob," retorted Angelo.

"Are you guys always at each other?" asked Marianna.

"Nah, we just bust each other's balls, Marianna," replied Sonny. "It's just our way. It takes practice to be good at bustin' somebody's chops."

Marianna shook her head in dismay. Angelo tossed a pillow at Sonny.

"Hey, what kinda host am I?" said Angelo. "Let me give you a tour and show you your room. You can freshen up after the long plane ride."

"And then we can go get some supper," added Sonny. "I'm getting hungry."

"You're always hungry, Sonny," said Angelo with a smile.

Angelo showed Marianna to the guest room, a tastefully decorated open space that overlooked the hustle and bustle that occurred on the street, complete with its own bathroom. Marianna was impressed. In some ways, it reminded her of places she had seen in West Hollywood.

After settling in, they walked over to Osteria Morini's, where they were welcomed with open arms. Hugging was common. Everyone seemed to know Angelo and Sonny as well as their families. Greetings were given in both Italian and English. When they sat down at the table, they didn't even have to order. Within a few minutes a bottle of Chianti was opened, poured, and the food began to arrive: multiple courses and small plates. Marianna sat in amazement as she gawked at the vast array of Italian delicacies that included bruschetta, mussels, and caprese, among others.

"Do you guys always eat this way?" asked Marianna in wide-eyed wonder. "It's enough to feed an army!"

"Nah, only when we come here," said Angelo. "Morini and our grandfather go way back to the old country. So anytime one of us comes in, they treat us like family."

"Family?" said Marianna. "More like royalty!"

"We also do business with the restaurant," added Sonny, "so one hand washes the other, so to speak. That's what family is all about, ya know."

La famiglia, thought Marianna. *La cosa nostra.*

"What kind of business are you into?" asked Marianna. "Do the two of you work together?

"Yeah, we're partners," replied Angelo. "We are in a family business. All of us work together. We provide private trash collection and security to wholesale and retail businesses in Manhattan and Brooklyn."

"My mother," said Sonny, "is a bookkeeper. My father, Dominic, is a project manager in the security business. As you know, my mother and Angelo's father are brother and sister. They are your father's – Tony's - sibs. Angelo and I grew up together, so we're more like brothers than cousins."

"That's why we're so good at bustin' each other's balls," exclaimed Angelo, giving Sonny a friendly shove.

"My father is also in the business and so is Aunt Lena's husband, Vinnie," said Sonny. "Grandpa Louie had four kids: Tony, Mike, Anne-Marie, and Lena. They are all married with kids. You'll meet them all tomorrow."

The waiter came by their table and poured more wine, opening another bottle as well.

"Tell us about Tony," said Sonny. "We haven't seen him since we were kids."

"He's my godfather, ya know," said Angelo. "I'd like to get to know him."

"The truth is," began Marinna, "I hardly know him. I only met with him twice and only learned about him a couple of months ago."

"It must have been weird, discovering you had another father and all," said Angelo as he took a bite of caprese. "I mean, like, walking into a room and, wow, there he is."

"Weird is an understatement," replied Marianna, taking a sip of wine. "I mean, up until a few months ago I didn't even know whether he was alive. And then, bam, one day I'm standing in front of him. I now have a *bio-dad* as well as a dad." She shook her head incredulously.

"I can only imagine," said Sonny. "We hadn't heard from him for around twenty years and then suddenly out of nowhere we get a call saying that he has a daughter who wants to meet us. And then we all saw the trailers for your TV show. First time we've seen Tony since he left New York."

"A real shocker, huh? Seeing Tony and meeting me," said Marianna. "You can imagine what it must have been like for Tony. Here's a forty-nine-year-old dude, living the quiet life of a construction guy with a wife and a daughter, when out of the blue, he's got a second grown-up kid."

Angelo and Sonny both nodded as they shoveled pasta into their mouths.

"What did you think of the trailer?" asked Marianna.

"I don't think any of us would have even seen it if it hadn't been for Tony's call telling us about you," answered Angelo. "I think it was Carla who saw it first. She's the TV addict in the family. It was even more weird for our parents, seeing Tony after so long."

They all fell silent, focusing on their food as they contemplated the unusual situation.

Marianna broke the silence. "So what happened that caused Tony to stop contact with the rest of his family?"

Angelo looked up from his pasta Bolognese. "What did he tell you?" he asked. A piece of spaghetti hung from the corner of his mouth.

"Not much," replied Marianna. "He simply said that he didn't want to take over the family business and Grandpa Louie, being old school, got pissed off and threw him out. So, he moved to California."

"That's pretty much the story we got," said Sonny, looking at Angelo for confirmation. Angelo nodded his head, wiping sauce off his mouth with a napkin.

"But why would he not have contact with his brother and sisters? Or you guys?" she asked. "I mean, when you were all grown up?"

"What d'ya mean?" asked Sonny.

"I mean, after all, you guys could have stayed in touch with him if you wanted to, no?" replied Marianna.

Angelo and Sonny glanced at one another and then stared at Marianna. Neither of them seemed to know how to respond.

"Uh, I guess," began Angelo. "I remember things were pretty tense around the house back then. I was only five years old when Tony left, but there was lots of commotion for years after."

"Anytime Tony's name was brought up," added Sonny, "there were arguments. Grandpa didn't want anybody mentioning Tony's name around him. It wasn't until we were teenagers and after Grandpa's first heart attack that we were told that Grandpa had pretty much disowned Tony for not wanting to take over the family business."

"There's got to be more to it than that," said Marianna. "It's strange how old school parents make such a big deal over whether the first born wants to go into the family business. Or even what career path a kid takes. Did Grandpa Louie see the trailers?"

The waiters brought cannoli for dessert, along with cappuccino and limoncello.

"I dunno," replied Sonny. "Interesting question. I wonder whether anyone told him about Tony being on television and about you being his daughter. Our parents often keep things from him if they think it will upset him."

"Or at least they try to," added Angelo, chuckling.

"Everyone else saw the trailers," said Sonny. "And they think they're meeting a movie star."

They all laughed.

The cousins spent the rest of the evening getting acquainted. Angelo was not married; he enjoyed the single life despite the pressure he received on a regular basis from his mother. Sonny was divorced and lived in Brooklyn, right across the Williamsburg Bridge, only minutes from the city.

They gave her a briefing on some of the people she was going to meet the following day. Louie Donatello had four children: Tony, Anne-Marie, Mike, and Lena. Until Marianna came into the picture, Tony was the only one who didn't have any biological children of his own. Marianna wondered whether this played a part in why Louie was so angry at Tony. Not only did he leave the family business, but he didn't give Louie any grandchildren; at least none that he could acknowledge. *He knew I existed,* thought Marianna.

Anne-Marie was married to Dominic and had two children, Sonny and Rosalie; Mike was married to Rose and had two children, Angelo and Theresa; and Lena was married to Vinnie and they had two children, Carla and Junior. Marianna calculated that she would be meeting twelve family members - thirteen, if Grandpa Louie showed up.

Angelo and Sonny were very interested in knowing about Marianna. She gave them a synopsis of what it was like for her growing up in the suburbs of Oregon and now living in Los Angeles. Living in the suburbs was quiet and very white. Her main contact with diversity came from her inner-city escapades. It wasn't until she moved to LA that she saw interracial couples, all kinds of ethnicities, and lots of traffic. She told them about being married and living in the canyons. She left out the part about cancer. And at this point, she was not ready to tell them about her forays into the dark side of her personality.

They told her about growing up in the Bronx and life in a big, vertical city. Marianna was fascinated by the differences between their lives. She had always known life in a single-family residence in suburbia, while Angelo and Sonny had grown up on the streets of a vertical city. Marianna had read books, mostly crime novels, about life in an urban metropolis; but she had never met someone who actually lived there. Sonny and Angelo's life sounded like one of her novels. Except for her relatively short stint living her shadow side after her cancer surgery, Marianna felt like she had lived a very sheltered life compared to her cousins who lived on the street every day.

CHAPTER NINE

The next morning, Sonny arrived at Angelo's apartment at around eleven. Marianna and Angelo were waiting on the stoop as the big Escalade pulled up to the curb. They were expected at Sonny's parents' house in the Bronx for lunch with the expectation that they would remain through dinner. Sonny took the East River Drive up to the Major Deegan Expressway into the East Bronx. The Morris Park area was a mix of single family brick homes and apartment houses. The area was home to one of the largest populations of Italian-Americans in the state.

The neighborhood where the Sardano family lived was all single family, brick homes, as well. Sonny's mother, Anne-Marie Sardano, was standing by the front door when the three cousins arrived. She must have seen them drive up.

Anne-Marie was a short, stocky, olive-skinned, forty-seven-year-old woman with graying black hair tied in a long single braid that ran down the middle of her back. She stood at the door wearing an apron and sporting a wooden spoon in her hand and a broad, welcoming smile on her face. The boys greeted her with a hug and kiss and then introduced her to Marianna. Anne-Marie threw her arms around Marianna, exclaiming that she looked exactly like her father. Sonny's father, Dominic, and his sister Rosalie stood nearby. They both greeted Marianna warmly, giving her a hug.

The smells of garlic, basil, oregano and tomato sauce wafted through the front door as they walked into a very comfortably furnished living room. The overstuffed chairs and couch invited people to feel comfortable and at ease. There was nothing formal about the home. Family pictures adorned the mantel of the fireplace. Knick-knacks were on the tables. It was a lived-in home.

One by one Marianna was introduced to *la famiglia:* Angelo's parents, Mike and his sister, Theresa, Tony's sister Lena and her husband Vinnie, and their daughter, Carla, and their son, Junior. They were all very welcoming, greeting Marianna as a long lost relative – lost for twenty-eight years. Marianna felt relaxed and could feel her guard dropping. They all wanted to hear the story about how she found Tony. They found it amazing that after twenty-eight years she could locate him. They were also intrigued by the fact that a documentary was being made of her discovery.

Angelo was right: being with this group was like being in the movie *My Big Fat Greek Wedding.* Marianna struggled to keep up with the barrage of questions and to follow the conversations. There were inside jokes, teasing, and lots of laughter as well as an abundance of food. It was strange for Marianna to be the oldest of seven cousins, ranging in age from Junior, the youngest at seventeen, to herself; all looking alike. The family resemblance was unmistakable. For a few moments, she tuned out all the chatter and just looked around the large dining room table thinking, *this is my other family.* She smiled at the thought.

Carla interrupted her reverie. "Marianna, what's it like knowing you're going to be on TV?"

"Huh? Oh, well, I haven't given it a whole lot of thought," answered Marianna. "I've been so involved getting my head around having a *bio-dad* and a new family that I've not thought much about the idea that I'm going to be on national television. I mean, I have had TV and movie parts as an actress so it's not entirely new; but never playing myself."

"Well, I think it's cool," said Carla. "And I can say to my friends, 'hey, that's my cousin' when the program airs. Maybe I should ask for your autograph now, before you're famous."

Everyone laughed.

"Have you ever met any movie stars?" asked Junior.

Marianna smiled. "Yes. I was at a party with Tom Cruise and was in a made for TV movie with Angelina Jolie," she replied. "I don't get many parts, but I keep going for auditions. That's the way the business works. You go for lots of auditions and hope that one will be *the* one."

"Good thing you have a day job," said Angelo with a slight smile.

"Oh? What kind of work do you do?" asked Lena.

"Mostly I am a self-employed physical trainer and nutritionist," Marianna answered. "My husband and I also run a small animal shelter."

"I guess that's why you look so buff," said Rosalie. "I could use a trainer to help me get rid of a few pounds."

"More than a few," jabbed Junior, smirking.

"Shut up, dork!" snapped Rosalie. "I can still kick your skinny butt."

They all chuckled. *I guess busting balls starts young,* thought Marianna.

"You guys mind if I ask a couple of questions?" asked Marianna, glancing around the table.

All heads turned in her direction.

"Do you think I will get a chance to meet my grandfather?" she asked. "Angelo told me that Grandpa Louie rarely joins in family gatherings because he has not been well. I would be more than happy to go visit him, if only for a few minutes."

The mood at the table changed. No one spoke.

"What did Tony tell you about your grandfather?" asked Mike as he poured himself more wine.

Marianna decided that she would not disclose everything that she had learned from her parents or from Tony. She wanted to hear directly from them.

Marianna looked directly at Mike and calmly replied, "All that I know is that Tony and his father had a falling out many years ago when Tony decided that he didn't want to take over the family business. He left for California and Louie pretty much disowned him. That's all I know."

Mike took a sip of his wine nodding. "Yeah, well, that's pretty much the way it was," he began. "But today, at eighty, our father is not doing too well. Now it pains him every day that my brother does not keep in touch. Both of them are quite stubborn." He shook his head. "Anyway, I'll talk to Grandpa. If he feels up to it, I'll take you to him."

Marianna wondered whether any of the family knew the whole story about the pregnancy and Louie threatening her parents and paying them off. But she didn't think it would be a good time to bring up any of that.

"You said you had a couple of questions, Marianna," interjected Anne-Marie, smiling pleasantly.

"Oh, yeah, I did say that. But, right now, I can't remember what the second question was," said Marianna, flushing.

"Don't ya hate when that happens?" interjected Carla. "Sometimes there's something I want to say, but then it just disappears from my brain. Like poof, gone."

"That's what happens to airheads," quipped Junior.

They all laughed.

Marianna knew they were holding back. She couldn't figure out why none of them were in contact with Tony. Was it only about being loyal to Louie, or was it something about Tony? Why didn't Tony reach out over these years? Maybe Tony was right: one doesn't just leave the *mafia;* especially if you're the son of the capo. Part of Tony's exile included being cut off from the family. He was *persona non-grata.* And no one was willing to violate Louie Donatello's order. But Marianna didn't think this was the right time to press the issue.

The rest of the afternoon and evening went well enough for a first visit. The warm and welcoming feeling persisted throughout the day. It was a typical Italian family with lots of laughing, wine, and food. Marianna enjoyed meeting her new relatives. And when it was time to leave, they all expressed a desire to see her again before she headed back to the West Coast. Marianna was invited to Angelo's parents, Mike and Rose's, house for dinner the following Sunday. They told her that Sunday dinner was a tradition in the family and they rotated among the siblings each week; one week at Mike and Rose's house, another at Anne-Marie and Dominic's, and the following week at Lena and Vinnie's. Marianna was warmed by the invitation and the thought of spending more time with her new family. They hugged her goodbye.

As Marianna, Sonny, and Angelo were driving back to Manhattan, they chatted more about the family, including some of the stories about why her *bio-dad*, Tony, was no longer connected to anyone. Marianna was relieved that they brought it up, saving her from figuring out how she was going to do it. They told her that while it was true that their grandfather, Louie, had expected Tony to take over the family business, and Tony didn't want to, it wasn't that simple. Her cousins told her that Grandpa Louie was old school. He believed that the first-born son had an obligation to the father to take over – it was duty, not a choice. When Tony refused, Louie felt disrespected, and for a Sicilian, *rispetto* sonno *molto importante* (respect is very important). So, important that Grandpa Louie disowned his son. And in the process, the entire family was put in the awkward position of not being able to stay in contact with Tony for fear of disrespecting Louie and, of course, possibly suffering the same consequences.

It was just as Marianna had suspected. *No one wanted to disrespect Louie and lose favor – or worse, becoming persona non-grata just like Tony.*

As they were driving down Eastside Drive into Manhattan, Angelo received a text message. He showed it to Sonny and then turned to Marianna. He told her that they had a business emergency they must attend to and would have to drop her off to take a taxi or Uber the rest of the way.

"No way," said Marianna. "If I'm family, I should be permitted to go along on family business."

"You're kidding, right?" replied Angelo with an edge. "You don't get to do a ride along just because Tony is your, uh, 'biodad', as you call him!"

"Right," added Sonny. "We just met you; you ain't family – yet."

"I get that," responded Marianna. But she was irked. "Are you going on *la cosa nostra* business?" She stared at them both with a touch of pique, anticipating their reaction.

Angelo turned around to stare at her. "Huh? What the fuck do you know about *la cosa nostra*?"

Marianna glared at Angelo and took a deep breath. "Okay," replied Marianna, deciding to lay it out. "Here's the deal. I know that Grandpa Louie is a Mafia capo and that Tony didn't want to be groomed to take his place. That's why Tony left. He wanted out of the *business*."

Both Sonny and Angelo sat with their mouths open in a mild state of shock.

"Tony told you?" asked Angelo. "Why the fuck would he do that?"

"Yeah," said Sonny. "That's crazy. He must really trust you."

"Look, just because Tony doesn't want to be part of the family doesn't mean that I don't," said Marianna. "I don't feel the same way."

Angelo's pager went off again. He turned to Sonny.

"We gotta get going," said Angelo. "We gotta roll; and quickly!"

They didn't have the time to talk further and it was too late to drop her off. So, they took Marianna with them on their mission. Within ten minutes they arrived at a liquor store on 10th Avenue. Marianna stayed in the car. She watched as Angelo and Sonny were met by an elderly Asian man, who was frantic. His voice was loud and he waved his arms as he spoke. He said he was held up by a couple of Latino thugs who stole $1200 and took a case of whiskey and a case of cigarettes. Tony and Angelo asked the man for a description and whether he had a video of the guys. Marianna watched as they went into the back room to view the surveillance tape; they printed out a copy of their faces. Once done, they assured the man that he would be reimbursed for his loses.

Angelo and Sonny got back in the car and took off, leaving a patch of rubber on the asphalt. Marianna questioned them, but they didn't respond. The next stop was a bar in the Williamsburg area of Brooklyn across the Williamsburg Bridge not too far from where Sonny lived. El Chico Bar and Grill was a dingy, smoke-filled joint that played loud Mexican and Puerto Rican music. The patrons were mostly Latino. This time Marianna didn't stay in the car, despite Sonny and Angelo's commanding her to do so. She wanted to be where the action was happening. After Angelo and Sonny left to go inside the bar, she walked around to the back alley where she found the rear entrance. The door was unlocked.

Sonny and Angelo went inside and approached the bartender, Jesus. Jesus recognized them and knew they were connected. Angelo spoke in low tones and showed Jesus the picture. Jesus pointed to a pool table where two guys were shooting a game, laughing, smoking, and buying rounds. Angelo went in one direction toward one of the guys while Sonny circled around in another direction toward the other and came up behind him. Before a word was spoken, the Tasers held by Sonny and Angelo rendered the young men helpless. As the guys slumped over, Sonny and Angelo led them out of the bar through the back door. It looked like they were helping a couple of drunks.

Marianna watched the entire transaction from the hallway that led to the restrooms and out the back door. Before the four men got to the doorway, she left and hid behind a dumpster in the alley. She watched as Angelo and Sonny went through the two guys' pockets, taking all the cash and their car keys and binding their hands with plastic cable ties. Just as one of the guys on the ground regained consciousness, Angelo grabbed him by the throat.

"Hey, punk, what the fuck you doin' in Manhattan, asshole?"

"I ain't done nothin'!" said the young man in defiance.

"You ain't done nothin', eh?," sneered Angelo. "Then where the fuck you get all that cash to buy rounds, huh? And the bartender tells me that you sold him some booze and cigs!"

"They musta fell off a truck! I found 'em." He snickered.

Angelo punched him squarely in the face. Marianna heard the snapping of the cartilage in the man's nose. Blood spilled out. Still gripping the man's throat, Angelo did a more thorough search through his pockets and pulled out the remainder of the twelve hundred dollars he had taken from the liquor store.

In the meantime, Sonny had the other guy on the ground face down with a knee in his back.

"Listen to me, dickwad," said Sonny in almost a hiss. "You and your amigo over there are gonna go back to that liquor store that you ripped off and apologize to the Asian dude. And –"

"Fuck you! I ain't gonna do shit!" exclaimed the man as he struggled to free himself.

"Really?" said Sonny as he reached into his back pocket to retrieve a pair of pruning shears. "I think you'll do exactly as I tell you, shitface. You're gonna apologize and you and that spic friend of yours are gonna give the Asian five large by tomorrow night as compensation for his time and trouble and for the booze and smokes." As he spoke, Sonny placed the pruning shears around the man's pinky and began to squeeze. "Do you understand what I'm sayin', shit for brains?"

Realizing what Sonny was about to do, the man's face turned white and he began vigorously nodding his head. "Yeah, yeah, I understand. We'll do it. Tomorrow night. Five grand. No problem." Marianna could see the sweat bead up on his brow.

Seeing what was happening to his friend, the guy being held by Angelo joined in. "Hey, we're sorry, man. We didn't know the dude was a friend of yours. Just let us go. We'll get the money and we'll get it to him. Promise."

"You don't seem to understand," began Angelo, tight-jawed and speaking between his teeth. "You stay the fuck out of Manhattan and the Bronx. You want to do some shit, do it in Queens or Brooklyn. Anywhere but the Bronx or Manhattan. Comprende?"

Both guys nodded in agreement.

"Just to show you that we mean business ..." Sonny squeezed the pruning shears, as the guy screamed out in agony. Blood squirted from the man's hand as his pinky fell to the pavement. Sonny continued. "If we find out that you didn't deliver the five grand, it will be more than a finger that you'll lose."

The other guy wretched as he saw what happened to his friend. Marianna felt like doing the same. She turned her head away and was ready to heave. But, realizing that she had better get back to the car before Angelo and Sonny, she left her hiding place and jogged down the alley and around to the front of the bar where the car was parked. She sat in the back seat, trying to control the trembling that overcame her. She gulped air, controlling her nausea.

A few minutes later, Angelo and Sonny returned. Marianna asked them whether they'd completed their business. She saw there was blood on Sonny's shirt. Noticing that she was staring, Sonny looked down at his shirt.

"It must have been some rough business," wisecracked Marianna.

"Sometimes people we meet in our line of work - the security business -" replied Sonny, "become a bit unruly and need to be, um, contained. In the process, sometimes people get hurt."

They drove back to Angelo's apartment in silence.

After witnessing the violence, Marianna wondered what her next move should be. While she wanted to get know her grandfather, she now questioned the wisdom of becoming more embroiled in the family business. She questioned the idea of telling her cousins what she knew about Grandpa Louie. The romantic notion of being the granddaughter of a mafia don lost some of its appeal when she was confronted with a sample of their violence. Watching Sonny cut off a man's finger was a little too much. It pointed to the harsh reality of the so-called security business that was operated by the family. It was a protection racket, plain and simple. Small businesses paid for protection for doing business in crime-ridden areas where they could charge whatever the traffic would bear.

When Marianna did her research on organized crime before leaving for New York, she read mostly about the high-end aspects of the business; what the newspapers called the "new Mafia." She read about the corporate dealings where MBA graduates dealt with the accounting practices of illegal enterprises, money laundering, off-shore accounts, and casinos. She had not considered life on the streets where South American drug cartels operated, prostitution was a staple, and violence was an everyday occurrence. She had not thought about the turf battles between the U.S. Mafia-run distribution of drugs and the Columbian manufacturers and exporters of the drugs.

Was this something that she wanted to make a part of her life? To be sure, part of it sounded exciting and intriguing; very different from her middle-class life as a physical trainer back in LA. She loved the TV shows *Breaking Bad* and *Narco*. But this was reality.

For their part, Angelo and Sonny were thinking about how or what to tell the family about taking Marianna along on the call. They wondered what she'd seen and what she thought.

When they reached Angelo's apartment, Angelo took three beers from the refrigerator, opened them, and handed one each to Sonny and Marianna.

"Try cold water on it before it sits too long, Sonny," said Marianna, her head motioning toward his blood-splattered shirt.

"Huh?" replied Sonny.

"You might want to wash the blood off your shirt," she said, taking a pull on the beer bottle.

Sonny walked over to the kitchen sink and turned on the cold water.

"The private security business can be a little rough," said Angelo. "It is different from police security. We don't have to follow the same rules."

"Yeah," added Sonny with a note of sarcasm. "And we don't have to Mirandize the perps."

"The thing is," said Angelo, "shopkeepers in the low rent districts know that they can get immediate and effective protection from us that they wouldn't get from the police. They call and we respond."

"Are there any women in the business?" asked Marianna.

"Yeah, in the office, but not on the street," said Angelo. "Why?"

"I think it's something I'd like to get into," she replied. Marianna surprised herself. Until that moment she hadn't been sure which direction she was heading.

Both Angelo and Sonny stopped dead in their tracks and stared at her

"Seriously? Are you fuckin' kidding me?" exclaimed Sonny, chuckling in disbelief.

Marianna didn't respond. She just stared at them. She felt the same as she had back in high school when she was told she couldn't compete against the boys.

"First of all," began Angelo, "this isn't the kind of business that you fill out an application for and then go on an interview. It's a family business and you have to be invited."

"I thought I *was* family," said Marianna, glaring at them intently. "Maybe I could move to New York and start at the bottom. You guys could teach me the ropes."

Sonny and Angelo were stunned. They hadn't expected this. Neither had Marianna.

CHAPTER TEN

Marianna found herself continuing to ruminate about whether she wanted to join the family and become part of the infamous Mafia. She wasn't even sure that she would be allowed to become part of it. Just because she was the biological granddaughter of a capo didn't necessarily give her a ticket of admission. But on the off chance that she could become a *wiseguy,* would she – should she? Could she?

She surprised herself by even thinking about engaging in something illegal. She thought she had put that part of her life behind her and had become a by-the-book kind of gal. She was raised with a high moral standard and a progressive liberal attitude. Since becoming an adult the idea of harming others was anathema to her. So why was she considering becoming a part of this internationally-known mob? Tony had told her that once you become a part of the organization, they own you. The only way out was in a pine box. He had been lucky. Angelo had told her that it was not like filling out an application and going for an interview. One had to climb up through the ranks, starting at the bottom. The top rung of the ladder was becoming a *made-man* – killing someone. That both intrigued and terrified her.

What am I doing? Am I so bored with my life, she thought, *that I crave some sort of excitement? Am I trying to prove something? I know that Grant would never be a part of this.*

Am I willing to give up my marriage, my career, and the life I created? These questions plagued her, recycling through her brain in an endless loop of questions with no answers.

Marianna lived a relatively traditional life, especially by Los Angeles standards. In addition to her personal training business, she had a job as a director of an animal shelter, lived in a ranch-style home in the one of the many canyons in the San Fernando Valley, and had been married for five years to Grant, an architect. They had two dogs and a parrot. She considered herself a liberal Democrat on most issues and was particularly outspoken about animal rights. She would describe her marriage to Grant as better than average. Though not particularly exciting, it was very comfortable and fulfilling. She was content. In most respects, it was like the majority of her friends. They enjoyed watching movies together, had sex twice a week, and had a few folks with whom they socialized. They had decided early on in their relationship that, though they liked children, they wouldn't have biological children and were not keen on adoption. The animals were enough. They were her children.

Now, years after her adolescent adventures and her short, post-cancer foray into darkness, discovering that she was connected to a Mafia family re-awakened the dormant dark side of her personality. Rather than living vicariously through her novels and TV shows, she saw an opportunity to have hands-on experience in developing this suppressed – or perhaps just controlled – part of her personality.

One evening, Sonny and Angelo decided to take Marianna to a club for some fun and to blow off a little steam. They wanted to show her a little of New York's night life, millennial style. They arrived around eleven o'clock. There was a long line of hip looking, well-dressed and well-heeled twenty-something people waiting to gain admission. Sonny and Angelo led Marianna to the front of the line. A huge bear of a man, whom Marianna guessed to be over six foot five and around three hundred and twenty pounds stood at the front door. She could barely see the door behind his massive hulk. He wore a black suit over a black tee shirt that strained against his chest and biceps. A goatee, a shaved head, and a diamond ear stud completed the look. No one would get by him; nor would they even try.

Angelo walked up to him.

"Come stai, paisano?" said Angelo in Italian, his arms spread wide.

"Bene, goomba," replied the smiling giant, giving Angelo a bear hug. "How ya doin'?"

"What d'ya say?" said Sonny giving the big man a fist bump. "Long time no see."

"What brings you guys down here?" asked the big guy.

"Hey, Marianna, meet Tiny," said Angelo. "His old man and my dad are goombas from way back."

Marianna's small hand disappeared inside Tiny's baseball mitt-sized grip.

"Marianna is our cousin from LA, here for a visit," explained Angelo. "We're trying to show her our fair city. It's her first visit to the Big A."

"Welcome to the Big Apple, Marianna," said Tiny, smiling broadly. "Step inside and have a good time."

He stepped aside as he opened the door and ushered the three of them inside. Their senses were bombarded. The music blared, heavy on the bass. Black walls with flickering neon, flashing mirrored globes hung from overhead rafters, and the smell of cigarettes, weed, beer, and perfume mixed with colognes of every description. And, of course, sweat. Bodies were crammed on the dance floor, gyrating to the beat. This place made the clubs that Marianna had frequented in LA seem tame in comparison.

They wiggled their way through the throngs and headed over to the bar area. Everyone seemed to know Angelo and Sonny. The bartender nodded in their direction and within moments they were being led to a booth along the wall obviously reserved for VIPs. No sooner were they seated than one of the servers brought over a bottle of Cristal champagne in an ice bucket. He popped the cork and served them. The club was so loud that shouting was necessary just to be heard above the din. So instead of talking, Marianna had a glass of champagne – and half of a second – as she took in the sights. Shortly afterward, she simply got up and walked over to the dance floor and began to gyrate along with the throngs.

She was enjoying the freedom of being away from her responsibilities and gave little thought to the fact that she had a husband in Los Angeles. The drinks had loosened her up. Her husband, Grant, did not like to dance. He preferred to work in his shop and watch movies on their wide-screen TV. Marianna, on the other hand, loved to move. She could feel the music taking her to another place.

While she was on the dance floor, a couple of guys tried to hit on Marianna. When she refused to go off with them, things got a little rough.

"What, you stuck up or somethin'?" said the bigger of the two guys.

"Yeah, you too good for us, little lady?" said the other guy, making a grab for her waist.

Marianna simply looked at them and said, "Hey, boys, why don't you just leave me alone and dance with each other?"

The two guys didn't take the hint and began to move in on her.

Angelo spotted the tussle brewing on the dance floor and was about to enter the fray to rescue Marianna when she spun around and landed a powerful kick to one guy's head, laying him out on the floor. When the other guy tried to grab her, she crunched his nose with a forceful elbow and followed up with a knee to his groin. Blood poured out of his nose. The other dancers gave her a round of applause. Tiny, the bouncer from the front entrance, made his way through the crowd, grabbed the two guys quickly, and ushered them off the dance floor and out the front door. Angelo watched with wide-eyed amazement at seeing his petite cousin totally take out a couple of two hundred-pound guys, bringing them both to their knees. He smiled with a newfound respect for her and joined in the applause.

Marianna felt a rush like none she had ever experienced before. This was the first time she'd used her martial arts training in an actual physical confrontation. Up until then, she had only sparred within the confines of the dojo where she'd trained. She made her way back to the table where Sonny and Angelo were seated. They each gave her a high-five as she sat down and gulped down a glass of water.

"That was awesome," said Angelo. "Where the fuck did you learn to do that?"

"I've been training for years," replied Marianna. Her face was flushed and she could feel her heart racing with excitement. She wasn't even out of breath from the altercation. This was a pure adrenalin rush. She loved the feeling.

"Those two guys went down like sacks of potatoes," exclaimed Sonny. "Maybe from now on they'll think twice before playin' rough with chicks."

Marianna was psyched. "How do you guys feel when you, you know, rough someone up?" She searched their faces.

Angelo was first to reply. "I dunno; like it's just something I gotta do. It's business, ya know?"

"Yeah," replied Sonny. "No big deal. It's not much different than growing up in the Bronx. I mean, like - fighting, busting heads - it's just part of what we do."

Marianna was silent for a few moments. She picked up the bottle of champagne from the ice bucket that sat on their table and poured herself a glass. She took a sip.

"I liked it," she said calmly.

"What? The champagne?" replied Angelo. "At five hundred bucks a bottle..."

"No, the feeling," said Marianna in quiet tone. "I liked the snap of the guy's head when I kicked him. And the crunch of the other guy's nose. I liked kicking the shit out of them. I felt a rush. It was a turn-on." She looked up at them.

Both Sonny and Angelo said nothing. They looked at each other and just nodded, very slowly.

Marianna found it difficult to fall asleep that night. She replayed the experience from the club, reliving the dancing, the pulsating music, the gyrating, and the two guys hitting on her. She felt the rage; she felt the heat. She felt her body tensing up as she threw the hard roundhouse kick to the guy's head. There was no holding back, as she had been trained to do when sparring. This was all out. And then the elbow to the other guy's nose - the sound and feeling of breaking his nose thrilled her. She felt alive; she felt powerful. She felt the wetness between her legs. It didn't take long for her to climax.

CHAPTER ELEVEN

On the following Sunday, as promised, the family met at the home of Angelo's parents, Mike and Rose. Marianna was surprised to find Grandpa Louie sitting in the living room. When Marianna walked in, everyone – except Louie - stood up and applauded. Instead, Louie tapped his cane. Sonny and Angelo had already reported the incident that took place at the club where Marianna took out the two guys. Carla, the nineteen-year old daughter of Lena and Vinnie, looked at her in awe. Marianna blushed. Everyone wanted to hear the story all over again; but this time, directly from her. It was Marianna's moment.

Despite her discomfort with the attention, she went through the events of the evening, describing the scene and circumstances as she remembered them.

"Weren't you afraid?" asked Carla, her eyes wide open in admiration.

"To tell the truth, I didn't have time to be afraid," replied Marianna. "I just reacted. When these two goons grabbed me, I didn't think. I just, uh, did what I had been trained to do."

"What do you mean by 'trained'?" asked Rose.

"I've been studying and practicing martial arts for years," explained Marianna. "Ever since high school."

"Ya mean like in Karate Kid?" asked seventeen-year old Junior. His eyes were wide in awe.

"Yeah, something like that," replied Marianna.

"Kia!!" yelled Junior, jumping up and assuming a stereotypical karate pose. "Awesome!"

Everyone laughed, including Marianna.

"Do you think I could learn it, too?" asked Carla.

"Sure, it's a great confidence builder," replied Marianna. "Anyone can learn. And it's great exercise."

"Have you beat up guys before?" asked Mike.

Marianna smiled. "Maybe once, in third grade," she replied with a smile.

Mike chuckled. "I mean seriously, as an adult?" he asked.

"Nope; at least not out in the real world," answered Marianna. "I've sparred with guys many times in the dojo. I've competed against big guys and little guys. Sparring and competing is part of the training. But this was the first time it was for real. In the dojo, we're trained to pull our punches and not hit below the belt or in the face. I've always wondered whether I could do it on the street, if I had to." She paused. "Now I know." She was pensive for a moment, nodding her head at the thought.

"I sure wouldn't want to mess with you," said Angelo. "Especially after what I saw." He put his hands up in mock surrender. "No way!"

Everyone chuckled.

"Let's eat," announced Rose, changing the subject.

The entire family got up and moved from the living room into the dining room. Grandpa Louie didn't move from his chair. He smiled at Marianna and motioned for her to sit next to him. Everyone stopped in their tracks as Marianna walked slowly toward the eighty-year old patriarch of the family, whom she had never met.

Louie wore a black turtleneck sweater under a grey suit. He had piercing blue-green eyes behind black-rimmed bifocals and thinning grey hair. He kept one hand on his knurled wood black cane with a silver handle. He was soft-spoken, as though used to having people listen when he spoke.

"Ciao, la mia bella nipote," said Louie. "Capisci?" *Hello, my beautiful granddaughter. Understand?*

"Si, capisco," replied Marianna. "Como stai, mio nonno?" *Yes, I understand. How are you, grandfather?*

Louie laughed out loud. "Listen to this, everybody; my new granddaughter understands and speaks Italian!" He was beaming. "Where did you learn Italian? Not from your father, I know."

"I studied it in college. It's such a beautiful language," said Marianna.

"Yes, it is. Just like you, granddaughter," said Louie, his eyes welling with pride. "Help me to the table. And sit next to me. Rose's food is delicious."

Marianna placed her forearm under Louie's arm, helping him out of his chair. He held his cane in the other hand and together they walked into the dining room. As always, the table was covered with enough food to feed twice their number. Sonny filled the wine glasses placed next to each plate. Louie nodded toward the head of the table. Sonny pulled the chair out for him as he lowered himself into it. Marianna sat to his left and Angelo sat to his right. Mike sat at the other end of the table.

Louie leaned toward Marianna and whispered, "I hear that you want to work in the family business. Is that true?"

Marianna looked into his blue-green eyes and nodded. "Yes, it's true."

The platters of food were passed around the table, each person taking a good-sized helping. This was a family of eaters. Mike stood up, tapping the side of his glass with his fork, making a clinking sound. Everyone turned toward him.

"I want to make a toast to my pop and to his long-lost granddaughter, Marianna. *Benvenuto nella nostra famiglia.* Welcome to the family, Marianna. Salute!"

Everyone turned toward Louie and Marianna, glasses raised. "Salute!" they said in unison.

Louie wiped his mouth with his napkin. He looked over at Marianna.

"Why?" he asked.

"Why what?" replied Marianna.

"Why do you want to be in the family business?"

His question caught her by surprise. Angelo's ears perked up, his fork paused midway between his plate and his mouth.

Marianna thought for a moment. "The idea of being in a family-run business – I don't know; it has a lot of appeal. Makes me feel part of something bigger than just myself. It's an opportunity to connect with my family."

"You know what kind of business this is?" asked Louie. "Not your typical mom and pop shop. Capisci?" *Understand?*

Marianna nodded, looking at Louie directly. "Io capisco." *I understand.*

"What did your father tell you about the business?" asked Louie. He spoke in almost a whisper, but loud enough that Angelo and others who paid attention could hear.

Marianna wasn't sure how to reply. She didn't want to say too much, but she also wanted to engage her grandfather. "He didn't say much except that he didn't want to take over the business as the oldest son was expected to do. That's why he left New York to move out to the West Coast. Most of what I learned about the business was what I read on the internet." She looked across at Angelo, who made a slight shake of his head before eating his next bite.

"Did you tell your father that you wanted to join the business?" asked Louie, sipping his wine. "Did he approve?"

"No. He didn't want me to come to New York at all," replied Marianna without skipping a beat. "I told him that just because he walked away from his family doesn't mean I have to. I had to insist. That's when he called Angelo."

Louie nodded. He gazed into her eyes. From years of experience reading people – one doesn't live to eighty as a capo if you cannot size people up quickly – he knew that she was not telling him the entire story.

When Marianna suggested that she wanted to participate in the family business, Louie felt conflicted. On the one hand, he wanted very much to have his granddaughter be a part of the family. On the other hand, he wondered whether the business was the best thing for her. *She has not grown up in the world of la cosa nostra,* he thought. *She's lived a protected life; for her this is a novelty.* She was an outsider. And one that he just met for the first time. He told Marianna that he would think about it and let her know his decision in a few days.

When the family finished eating, the men moved into the living room while the women, including Marianna, cleaned up. This was the Italian way. Old school. Roles for men and women were clearly prescribed. It was not that women were thought of as weak; it was just that they were perceived as having different strengths. Their strength was running the family; they were behind the scenes. This was not the way that Marianna thought of herself. She knew that being an

117

active participant on the street like Angelo and Sonny was not going to be an easy sell to Grandpa Louie even if he accepted her into the family business.

The adult women – Anne-Marie, Rose, and Lena - as well as the younger women, Rosalee, Theresa, and Carla, chatted amiably with Marianna. The older women wanted to know more about what it was like to discover her birth father after so many years. The younger women were more interested in how she took down the guys in the club. They were impressed with how Marianna had integrated being feminine with being tough.

Marianna felt comfortable with all of them. She was particularly smitten by their candor. Every topic seemed to be fair game. They clearly had a voice and were more than willing to share their thoughts and opinions. It was quite different from the family in which she'd grown up, where opinions were rarely expressed.

"I can only imagine what it must have been like for you," began Anne-Marie, "meeting your biological father for the first time."

"Yeah, it was quite a shocker, seeing this guy who looked a lot like me," replied Marianna. She continued to dry the pots as they were handed to her.

"What about for Tony?" interjected Lena. "I mean, all these years thinking he would never have a child of his own and suddenly she shows up at age twenty-eight!"

"I guess it was more of a shock to him than to me," Marianna replied. "I have a dad, and never thought much about it. I mean, I was eighteen when I found out that I was adopted. I had a dad who was suddenly my adopted dad. Now, at twenty-eight, I got a biological father - a *bio-dad*."

"*Bio-dad*, that's funny," said Carla. "Makes a great book or movie title. I picture some kind of robot." She chuckled.

And so it went. The conversation was easy. The older women were interested in learning more about Marianna and what their brother, Tony, was up to; while the younger girls were interested in finding out whether Marianna knew any famous people in LA. Junior wanted to know more about the martial arts. She had a little something for everyone.

Just then, Mike entered the kitchen. "Pop - I mean, Louie - wants to talk with you," he said, looking at Marianna. Rose, Mike's wife, gave him a quizzical look, raising her eyebrows. Mike shrugged.

The women all gave each other a look. Marianna smiled at them, handed off her dish towel, and left the kitchen to go into the living room. Louie was seated in the same chair as when she'd first arrived. There was a vacant chair next to him. Louie motioned to Marianna to sit next to him, patting the chair.

"Vieni a sederti accanto a me la mia bella nipote," said Louie in Italian. *Come sit next to me, my beautiful granddaughter.*

Marianna sat down in the vacant chair. She felt like she was having an audience with the Pope.

Louie held his cane with both hands and leaned his chin on them. He continued to fix her with his gaze, waiting for her to talk. He knew she had something on her mind. He was right. Marianna wanted to know his side of the story about why Tony had disappeared from her life. She decided to tell him what she knew.

The words just tumbled out. She hardly took a breath. "My parents told me that Tony had seduced my mother, and that's how she became pregnant with me. She wanted to keep me, so my father stepped up and told everyone that he was the baby's father. However, through some slipup in the hospital, my mother's parents found out that this wasn't true. They hired an investigator, who located Tony and got a sample of his DNA. The test confirmed that he was my biological father. Tony was afraid that he would be charged with statutory rape. Somehow you found out about all of this – I guess Tony told you, and wanted your help. You stepped in and threatened to take me away from my parents. Eventually a deal was struck. You would not file for custody or harm me or them in exchange for my parents' silence. To seal the deal, you paid them off. That's all I know." She finally took a breath.

The rest of the family was spellbound by the story. They sat on the edge of their chairs, waiting to see how Louie would respond. They were surprised to see his eyes welling up with tears.

"It's true," he began. He spoke slowly and deliberately. "I wanted you to be part of the family. You were my first-born grandchild. Your father was a wild kid; always getting into trouble. He liked to drink and chase the skirts. I had hopes for him to join me in the business, but that wasn't to be. And, when I learned about you, I wanted you to come live with us. But I wasn't willing to go through a court battle. It wasn't good for business. So, I made the deal." He hesitated for several minutes before continuing. "I've thought about you often, wondering how you turned out." A tear rolled down his cheek. "And disowning your father was one of the most difficult decisions I've ever had to make. But that is our way. It was the best choice."

The family couldn't believe their eyes, seeing the tough old family patriarch showing such emotion. It was a very moving moment. All through their lives, Louie was the hard-as-nails *Godfather*, invoking fear in the hearts of everyone around him. Seeing his softer side was surprising. Louie now seemed like many eighty-year-olds dealing with the regrets of their past. For the first time, he seemed vulnerable. He seemed human.

Marianna reached out and put her hand on top of his. Suddenly, as though coming out of a trance, Louie's mood changed. His penetrating blue-green eyes turned cold. The shift of his mood was palpable. The steely *Godfather* had returned as he sat upright in his chair. The tears were gone.

"I'll let you know about the business as soon as I've decided," he said. He pushed down hard on his cane and stood up. "Michael, it's time; take me home." The audience was over.

CHAPTER TWELVE

L ater that night, as Marianna lay in bed, she thought about Louie and how quickly his moods could change. One moment he was a kindly old grandfather and the next he was the cold, remote head of a Mafioso family. She imagined what he must have been like as a young man. The thought made her shudder. That was the mercurial man Tony had grown up with; that was the father who had disowned him. That was the man who threatened her parents. 'That is our way' he had said. No regrets.

The internal debate over whether she truly wanted to become a part of *la famiglia,* even if Louie gave his consent, continued to rage in her mind. She knew that it wouldn't be a walk in the park. She would be required to do things to people – to hurt people – in ways that she would be taught to be cruel. She would be participating in a world outside the law. She would be a criminal, and if she got caught, she would go to jail. *La famiglia* was organized crime, and Louie was a *crime* boss. The loving family that she just met was involved in a *crime* syndicate. She wondered whether they gave it any thought. How did they reconcile their Catholic faith with the fact that they were condoning, as well as participating in, acts of violence and illegal activities? This was a question that often plagued her when watching movies and television shows. History suggested that the Catholic Church turned a blind eye toward the mafia. They took the donations and gave absolution. She wondered whether priests struggled with the hypocrisy.

Marianna considered whether she could discuss this with any of them. Did they even think of these issues? How was she going to reconcile it, herself? They all seemed like such good people, yet they were doing very bad things. Marianna knew that, for her to become one of them, she would have to do bad things; she would have to learn how to compartmentalize, separating her light and dark sides and become a Jekyll and Hyde character. She would have to be one person by day and another by night. *Can I do that? Can I make it just business? Do I want to?* With these thoughts on her mind, Marianna fell into a restless sleep.

Louie met with the family to decide on the best approach to take. His second son, Mike, was the next in line to take over the business when Louie died. Louie was still old school when it came to delegating power. While Anne-Marie was older by birth, she was a female. Females couldn't become capos. Louie knew of one exception. One woman had taken over her husband's organization when he died, but she had to make her son the spokesman; he sat at the table, not her. None of the older capos would negotiate with her. But she held the power. That presented Louie with another problem. There were no females working the street. Women remained in the background, taking care of operational and administrative matters. How could he put Marianna on the street? Would she be respected? After hearing how she'd handled herself in the club, everyone knew that she could handle herself in a fight. But fighting is different from breaking bones or using a gun, when necessary. Did she have the balls? Whether she could handle the types of situations she would inevitably confront in the business remained to be seen.

After the meeting, it was decided that Marianna would be given a trial run over the next week or two. Angelo and Sonny would be told to include her in some of the family business. They were to be her mentors. Marianna would be tested. This was a very unusual situation. The uniqueness of Marianna's sudden appearance on the scene made it necessary to come up with a unique solution.

Meanwhile, Marianna had called Grant, telling him that she intended to stay in New York for another two weeks. He was none too pleased, but he knew better than to press her. He figured there would be time enough for him to push-back later. In the meantime, he would do what he often did – wait. Marianna didn't tell him that she had hoped Louie would let her become active in the family business. Though she wasn't sure that she was willing to make a lifetime commitment to being an active member of the syndicate, she knew that she had to experience first-hand what it was like. She didn't want to have any regrets for not taking the opportunity. She thought of it more like being an undercover cop, like those that she read about in novels. She neglected, however, to think of what regrets she might have for things she might have to do. She forgot that regrets come in two forms: acts of omission and acts of commission.

When Mike told Angelo and Sonny that they would be responsible for taking Marianna under their wing for the next week, they were not too happy. It felt like baby-sitting; mostly because she was a girl. They would not have felt the same if Marianna were male. Despite their youth, they too were old school. Guys had to look after gals; even tough ones like

Marianna. The decision had been made, however. They had to follow orders. It was their job, now, to tell Marianna.

The day after hearing the family's decision, Sonny and Angelo decided that they would meet up at Angelo's apartment and tell her together. They recognized that Louie was making decisions a lot faster than when he was younger. He used to be more deliberate, often taking weeks to decide on important changes. He would look at things from all sides, using the perspicacity he had developed during his rise within the organization. Now that he was in his eighties, he seemed to make more rapid decisions, as though he felt the pressure of time to settle things quickly. Both Angelo and Sonny, as well as other members of the family, thought his decision to include Marianna in the family business wasn't one of his best ones. Mike even wondered whether the old man was losing it.

***

It was a rainy morning in New York: a Spring shower. Marianna stood by the window, watching the rain. She found it fascinating how people in New York were not deterred by the weather. They simply grabbed an umbrella, donned their raincoats, and went about their business. In Los Angeles, where it rarely rained, the streets would be devoid of foot traffic at the slightest shower. There weren't many pedestrians in general in Los Angeles, but when it rained, there were even fewer. The open-air malls would be virtually empty.

She and Angelo were having a cup of coffee when the doorbell rang. Angelo answered and let in Sonny, who was carrying a bag of warm bagels.

"Hey, cuz, how you doin'?," said Sonny in his customary laid-back style.

Marianna tried to imitate his New York accent. "Hey, I'm doin' good. How you doin'?" They all laughed.

Sonny poured himself a cup of coffee and took a bagel out of the bag. Angelo grabbed a plate and laid out the bagels. He took a container of cream cheese out of the refrigerator and a knife from the drawer and put them all on the coffee table.

Marianna smiled. "Those bagels smell so good," she said. "In LA we rarely have fresh bagels, except when we go to a deli. Otherwise, we pick them up in the supermarket; but they're not the same."

"New York bagels are the best," said Angelo, cutting one open and spreading some cream cheese on it. "This is called a 'schmeer'. Bagel with a schmeer. Delish!"

Sonny put down his coffee cup. "We got some business to discuss," he began.

"Yeah," said Angelo, looking at Marianna. "The family has been discussing your wanting to join the family business."

"Yeah, and?," she replied. "I've been waiting for Grandpa Louie to give it the okay." Marianna looked back and forth between her cousins.

"Louie gave his okay – at least for the time being," said Sonny. "He made Angelo and me your mentors."

Marianna gave a nod, hiding her pleasure. "You guys don't seem too happy about it. What's up?" she asked.

Angelo and Sonny stared at her. "Why should we be happy about it?" asked Angelo. "I mean, no offense, but here you come outta nowhere, and before you know it, you're in *la famiglia*. It's not right. Louie's losin' it or something. It doesn't make any sense."

"Yeah," added Sonny. "And here we are, stuck with babysitting you. It's not enough that we gotta watch each other's backs; now we gotta watch yours. You didn't grow up on the streets or in the business. What the fuck do you know? Nuthin', that's what!"

Marianna felt her eyes welling with tears. She hadn't expected harshness from her cousins. And the last thing she wanted to do now was show them any weakness. She gritted her teeth and stared at the carpet, focusing hard to fight back the tears. She looked up, mustered her resolve, and glared at them. She also knew that she would have to respond in a way to show her cousins that she had the grit to make it on the seamy side of life.

"I fuckin' get it, guys. I get it," she replied. "I'm a girl from LA. I don't know shit. You're right. I don't know dick about life on the street or how things work around here. But I can take care of myself, and I'm a quick study. And I am a member of this family and I will earn your, and everyone else's, respect." She held their gaze. She was not going to be dissuaded.

They just sat without saying a word. Finally, after a few moments, Marianna reached across the coffee table for a bagel. She cut it in half, put a schmeer of cream cheese on it, and took a large bite as if this was business as usual and the deal was done.

Angelo smiled. "I guess that's that."

"You're one spunky bitch, cuz," said Sonny. "I'll give you that." He snatched the other half of Marianna's bagel and bit it in half with one bite.

"So what do we do now?" asked Marianna, feeling relieved.

"I guess the first step is for us to explain what we do and how we do it," answered Angelo.

"And then I suppose we gotta introduce you around," added Sonny. "You gotta meet the people we protect – our clients."

Sonny and Angelo proceeded to tell Marianna how the family's loan, security, and enforcement operations worked and what their responsibilities were. They explained that the loan business entailed lending money to people who had no credit and nowhere else to turn. The people who availed themselves of this form of cash were desperate and couldn't get funds from legitimate sources. Usually the loans were short term; primarily because the *vig* (interest rate) was so high. Sonny and Angelo would arrange for the loan and its subsequent collection. When someone defaulted on a loan, it was Sonny and Angelo's responsibility to dish out the consequences both to encourage payment and to deliver a message to others that they would be held accountable for their debts. They were enforcers.

The security business was a protection business. Storekeepers paid the family a monthly fee to both insure that they would not be robbed and, if they were, to know that the criminals would be punished and would have to make restitution. Traditional security companies would only attempt to prevent a crime, but would not track down the perpetrators - they worked in conjugation with law enforcement. The family business involved being protector, investigator, and enforcer all in one. In addition, the business used pressure tactics to gain new business. They would create the crime to show the proprietor why their protection services were required. Thus, often the shopkeeper was paying to be protected from the family itself.

A big part of the family business was the creation of gambling enterprises and the protection of independent bookies, who paid the family a percentage of their take for protection and collection. Bookies took bets on anything from sporting events to politics. As long as there were gamblers, there were bookies. And bookies needed protection. The enforcement business primarily involved working with bookies who were being stiffed by gamblers who built up big debts and did not pay them off. Since bookies had illegal betting operations, the bookie could not go to the police. Nor could the gambler. The bookie kept the family on a retainer and paid the family a percentage of the debt that was recovered.

These operations all required both muscle and street smarts. They were the lowest rung of the family business. While the family used to be involved with marijuana, the development of medical marijuana dispensaries and the legalization of pot in some states took that off the table. The family did not want to get into the crystal meth business, claiming that the users and suppliers were too crazy to deal with. They left that business to the Mexicans and Asians.

"In short," said Angelo, "we're dealing with the rough side of the business. Our parents keep their hands clean. They can wear suits." Angelo chuckled. "We get our hands dirty."

"Yeah," added Sonny, "we deal with the messy side. You already saw how messy it can become when we went to Brooklyn."

Marianna nodded. Despite what she'd seen, she was totally captivated by the scope of the business and could hardly wait to start working. She tried to talk herself out of it, realizing that she was about to cross a line. But she was hooked.

"Have you ever handled a gun?" asked Sonny.

Marianna's eyes opened as wide as saucers. "You mean, like a pistol?"

"Yeah, like a pistol...any handgun," said Sonny.

"Uh, no; I've never handled a handgun," she replied. "I fired a shotgun once when a friend took me skeet shooting."

Sonny reached into the back of his waistband, with his right hand, pulled out a Glock 19. Marianna was startled, sitting back in her chair. Sonny quickly removed the clip and ejected the bullet sitting in the chamber. He handed the weapon to Marianna who held it tentatively in both of her hands. She was surprised by its heft, thinking that it was heavier than she'd expected. The longer she held it, the more comfortable she became. She liked the feel of the steel in her hand. Holding the weapon sent a thrill through her body. Marianna held it with two hands, as she had seen on TV, sighting down the barrel.

"When are you going to teach me how to use it?" she asked. "No sense holding it without learning what to do with it." She tried to sound nonchalant.

"All in due course," replied Angelo. "One of these days we'll take you somewhere where you can practice."

"Why not a range?" she asked.

"Can't go there with a nonregistered gun and no license," replied Sonny, staring at Marianna. "This isn't a sport, cuz. It's business." He put out his hand. Marianna handed him the Glock.

CHAPTER THIRTEEN

T he three cousins spent the next several days driving around the city. Marianna got to see parts of Manhattan and the Bronx that she never would have seen on her own. Angelo and Sonny took her to the racetrack in Yonkers in the northern section of the Bronx where she met some of the bookies, and inside the casino located at the track where she met pit bosses, loan sharks, and other assorted characters. In the South Bronx, an area known as Fort Apache, she saw drug deals being made and people shooting up out in the open. Even the police kept a respectable distance. At night, she heard gunfire. The only place in the Bronx that seemed safe was a small section known as Little Italy, over on Arthur Avenue. It was a protected area owned and operated by Italians and had remained that way for several generations.

It was strange for Marianna to see a borough so divided. She observed the same thing in Manhattan. One could see the upscale areas where the upper middle class and uber-rich lived, while a few blocks away, drug deals were being made.

In Harlem, the upper part of Manhattan, she met African-American store owners, drug dealers, bar owners, massage parlor owners, check cashing shops, and pimps. All these people either worked for the organization or were under its protection.

Down in Lower Manhattan, Marianna was introduced to doormen who were on the payroll for keeping an eye and ear open. They also served to make introductions to people who could be good for business. The shopkeepers on the Lower East Side and West Side were clients. Gang leaders knew the rules and how the turf was divided. They knew what they could and could not do on the street. When they met Marianna, they were both surprised and uncomfortable because she was female. In their culture, women belonged at home. They couldn't imagine taking orders from a woman. They needed convincing, but the best convincing would happen when they saw Marianna in action. She would have to earn their respect, and that wouldn't be easy.

It became obvious to Marianna that *la famiglia* had a long reach. Manhattan and the Bronx were big territories.

One night Angelo received a call from one of the pimps in Harlem.

"Hey, you gotta get over here quick," began the caller. "Some mothafucka is trying to horn in on my action! He's been threatin' my girls. You betta take care this shit now!"

"Chill, baby, we're on our way," replied Angelo. "Where are you now?"

"You just show up. I'll find you!"

Angelo, Sonny, and Marianna got in the Escalade and sped up the Westside Drive to Harlem in under thirty minutes. Midnight traffic was light. When they reached the corner of 7th Avenue and 125th Street, the street was busy. Harlem rarely slept. No sooner had they pulled into a parking space when there was a banging on the driver's side window. An angry, skinny black man with a slim mustache and a diamond stud in his left ear began giving Angelo and Sonny an earful.

"I'm gonna cut that mothafucker into small fuckin' pieces if you don't take care of this, Sonny. I'm payin' you, man!"

"Don't worry about it, Farrokim," replied Sonny, speaking calmly. "What does the dude look like and where do you think we can find him?"

"He looks like a linebacker," exclaimed Farrokim. "Big dude. Bald with a gold tooth right in front. Goes by the name of Jamal. He drives around in a big, old, silva Rolls. Man is all flash. Gives the workin' pimp a bad name. Hangs out around 123rd in a club called Big Mama's."

"We'll pay Jamal a visit," said Sonny as he pulled away from the curb.

"How do you want handle this, Sonny?" asked Angelo.

"I think we should just go have a talk," replied Sonny. "Maybe this Jamal doesn't know how things go. Maybe he needs a little education. We can always come back with some additional muscle."

How can they be so casual about this? thought Mariana. *We're three whites going into a black club in a tough neighborhood, up against a linebacker. No doubt he has a crew.* She could feel the adrenalin begin to course through her veins.

"How ya doin', Marianna?" asked Angelo with a half-smile.

"How do you think I'm doin'? I'm pumped," she replied. She used to have similar feelings when she was about to enter a karate competition.

A few minutes later they pulled into a parking space a few doors down from Big Mama's. Big Mama's had a neon flashing image portraying a large woman shaking her hips and sporting a beckoning smile. They noticed the silver Rolls Royce parked in front. The heavy bass from the music flowed into the street. A few people stood outside, smoking and gyrating. They stared at the odd threesome walking toward them. Standing in front of the entry, blocking their way, was a heavily muscled, dark-skinned guy in a black T-shirt with the name 'Big Mama's' written in white across the front image of a large-hipped, smiling woman.

"Wha' chu want here?" said the big man, jutting his chin out; his arms folded across his chest.

"Came to see Jamal," said Sonny. "He here?"

"Who's askin'?"

"Just tell him that some friends of Farrokim want a word with him," said Sonny.

"Wait here," said the big man.

A few moments later the big man returned. He held the door open and motioned with his head for them to go inside.

So far, so good, thought Marianna.

Inside, the music was even louder. Conversation was all but impossible. From somewhere behind them they heard a voice telling them to just walk toward the back where they saw, facing them and sitting in a booth, the big, bald head and the flash of a gold tooth. When Jamal saw them, he stopped talking and gave them a big smile. When he spoke, his voice was deep and resonant.

"I hear you white folk want to talk with me," said Jamal. "So go ahead and talk. You've got three minutes."

Angelo stepped forward, leaning his hands on the table. "My name is Angelo. These are my cousins, Sonny and Marianna."

"Have we met before?" asked Jamal. Up close, Angelo could see a small diamond in the center of the gold tooth.

"No, Jamal. We haven't, and I hope we won't have to meet again. My family – the Donatello family – we have a special relationship with Farrokim. I believe you know him. He tells me that you've been, uh, interfering with his business."

"I don't know you or your family," said Jamal contemptuously. "And I really don't give a shit. I suggest that you turn your white asses around and get the fuck outta here before somebody gets hurt."

"I don't think you understand, Jamal," replied Angelo calmly. "You must be new around here. Maybe you oughta ask around about my family before you go get yourself hurt. Know what I'm sayin'?"

Jamal started to stand up, but Angelo put his hand on the man's shoulder and pressed down. Marianna stepped in closer. One of the men sitting at table placed his hand on Marianna's chest to push her out of his way. She quickly grabbed his wrist in a lock, forcing his head onto the table. She prepared to strike his throat. Angelo gave a quick shake of his head, stopping her. Sonny had already made the Glock visible.

Angelo continued. "Just check around before you go any further with your plans to interfere with Farrokim. Let me just tell you, should you decide to proceed, we'll be back. You feel me?" He stared menacingly at Jamal.

And with that, they walked out of the bar. Conversation over.

Once back in the car, Marianna asked, "So what was that about? I thought we were supposed to rough him up or something."

"You watch too much television, cuz," replied Angelo. "Most of the time we don't have to resort to violence. It's pretty much a last resort."

"But what about those guys the other night?"

135

"Those two guys were wannabes," replied Sonny. "They were trying to get noticed; make a mark. They wanted some gang to recruit them. We had to discourage that shit."

"But Jamal, here; he is a high roller with a crew," added Angelo. "We were on his turf. All the guys around there were packin'. We wouldn't have survived. It was a lot wiser to deliver a message and leave. We wanted to make sure that they understood there would be consequences and there would be payback. I'd rather assume they didn't know any better. Now they know. They'll ask around. Maybe they just played with Farrokim to bring about a meeting with us; to let us know that there was another player on the field. Two possibilities. Now we wait and see what their next play is."

"Geez. This is a lot subtler than I would've thought," said Marianna, shaking her head. "It never would've occurred to me that they might be making a statement and wanted to meet."

"Like I said," replied Angelo, "you watch too much television. The days of shoot 'em up in the street are over – at least in our business. The blacks and Puerto Ricans have at it like that every once in a while, but that's not how we generally operate."

"So what's with the Glock?" asked Marianna.

"Protection and intimidation," said Sonny. "And it doesn't mean that we don't occasionally have to resort to more conventional techniques. But when we do, it is all calculated to have the greatest impact with the least risk."

"What happens if Jamal continues to interfere with Farrokim's business?" asked Marianna.

"Then we'll know exactly where Jamal stands," answered Sonny. "We'd begin by finding who is involved in their crew and what else he's into. We might set him for a bust by NYPD. Or we might reduce the size of his crew, one by one. Or maybe we make him an offer he can't refuse. Between now and then, we'll collect intel on him, so we're ready."

"But what about Farrokim?" asked a confused Marianna. "Doesn't he expect some immediate satisfaction?"

"We'll have a chat with Farrokim," replied Angelo, "once his high wears off. He'll go along with the long game and will keep us filled in on developments with Jamal."

***

During the next several days Marianna accompanied Angelo and Sonny as they carried out their daily routines. It was not nearly as exciting as she'd expected. Most of their time was spent schmoozing with bartenders, pimps, storekeepers, bookies, and an assortment of other folks with whom they did business. In each of these places an envelope was passed between them containing the weekly payments. It was an all-cash business. And business was good.

The best part of daily rounds was meeting people that she would otherwise never have the opportunity of meeting. Each one of the people she met had a story to tell. Sometimes her cousins filled her in, other times she was able to engage the folks directly. As Angelo and Sonny introduced her to these people, Marianna became a little less interested in the business and more interested in the people. She met Liza, a single mother of two young children with a grade school education, who'd turned to prostitution to support her babies. She met a Muslim family from Afghanistan who ran a small mom and pop grocery store in a seedy part of town. They worked fifteen or more hours a day, sometimes sleeping in the back of the shop, trying to eke out a living to support their three children. They needed protection from the druggies, the alkies, and general hoodlums who hung out in the neighborhood and perceived them as an easy mark. The police were too busy elsewhere in the city to pay attention to the little people who were struggling to survive. And *la famiglia* looked after them – for a price. One of the main differences between *la famiglia* protection and police protection was that *la famiglia* almost always got the stolen property or cash returned. And, unlike with the police, their protection was feared by the hoods.

On occasion when Sonny and Angelo had to use physical force to deliver a message, Marianna found herself feeling sorry for some of the recipients of the message. Some were simply bad dudes and deserved punishment, but others were just trying to get by. In this world, the underbelly of urban life, it was difficult to differentiate the good guys from the bad. For Angelo and Sonny, it was always just business. They didn't have to judge. But this was not the case for Marianna. She could not suppress either her empathy or her humanity. Both attributes could render her ineffective and could even put her in danger.

One evening Angelo received a call from a bookie claiming that he needed an enforcer to take care of a deadbeat who had been stringing him along on a twenty-five-thousand-dollar debt. The bookie wanted his money and wanted to teach the deadbeat a lesson.

Angelo, Sonny, and Marianna drove to greasy spoon diner in Chinatown to meet the bookie and get a description of the deadbeat. The bookie, Dino "The Elf" Mascolo, was in his mid-forties, just under five feet tall, and weighed about ninety pounds. He had been a jockey back in the day, but a mean fall off a balking horse had left him physically disabled and ended his career. But he understood track odds, knew horses, and loved action. Becoming a bookie was natural for him: he could then monetize his expertise. But being so small and slight, he also needed protection. Bullies were in abundance. Everyone thought they could take advantage of him. The family's job was to make sure that everyone knew that The Elf was being protected.

"Hey, Elf, how's it going?" said Angelo as they approached.

Elf was smartly dressed, wearing a black open-collared shirt, slim-fitting sport jacket, black jeans, very shiny black boots, and a fedora. He looked like he'd stepped out of GQ magazine. Or like he was a miniature of TV's Ray Donovan.

"Can't complain," said Elf, "except for this dickwad who's trying to stiff me for twenty-five large. Who's the chick?" He grinned as he gave Marianna a once-over with his eyes. Marianna was just a couple inches taller than Elf.

"This is our cousin, Marianna," replied Sonny. "She's the newest member of the family."

The Elf tipped his hat. "Pleasure to meet you, sweetcakes." Marianna shook his extended hand and smiled, with a nod.

"So what's the story on the deadbeat?" asked Marianna taking the lead. "How'd he get into you for twenty-five grand?"

"Just like the rest," answer Elf. "He started out small; a little here, a little there. He'd always pay it off within a few weeks. Then his bets got bigger and so did his debt. He began to ask for extensions. His debt got larger than usual, but not over the top. Then one day he says he's got a sure thing going on. He knew a guy who told him that the fix was in on a middleweight fight over in Jersey and he could score big. I'd heard of the fighter and knew some of the players. I thought he might be legit. So, I fronted him the money. The fighter lost. No such thing as a shoo-in. The next thing I know, the dude makes like the wind and blows. You guys gotta find him and let him know he never should fuck with The Elf."

"What do you know about him?" asked Angelo. "Where does he work, where does he live, where does he hang out? Is he married? Tell us what you got, Elf."

Elf gave Marianna his most charming smile. He was clearly attracted to her.

"Elf, pay attention," said Angelo. "You want this guy and your money? Or do want to stand around here gawking at Marianna's tits? Give us what you got."

Elf turned, his face becoming serious. "Okay. He a fifty-something-year-old white dude who sells Porsches over on 11ᵗʰ Avenue. His name is Walter Esterbrook. He's married to a broad who likes to live large, spending more than he brings home. He tries to supplement his income and satisfies his need for excitement by fancying himself as a high roller. He's got one kid in a private school. That's it; that's what I know."

"What does he look like?" asked Marianna.

Elf turned back to Marianna, again giving her a wink. "He's tall; but everyone is tall compared to us, eh, sweetcakes? Around six feet. Grey hair and a grey beard. How about going for a drink with me, sweetcakes?"

Marianna looked at him, giving Elf her most winning smile. "Thanks for the invite, Mr. Elf, but since I'm married, I'll take a pass."

Elf's smile turned to a fake pout. "So you don't fool around on the side? Even with handsome devil like me?" He chuckled.

Marianna shook her head. "Sorry. No, but thanks."

The three of them turned and walked back to the van. As they drove away, Sonny said, "Ya know, I think the Elf's got the hots for you, cuz."

"That type's got the hots for anything in a skirt," replied Marianna.

"You're probably right," said Angelo, chuckling. "Okay: first stop, the Porsche dealer. We gotta have a conversation with Mr. Walter Esterbrook."

"Ya know, Sonny," said Angelo, "I think we oughta let Marianna take the lead on this one. Let's see how she is able to show Walter the error of his ways."

"Good idea," exclaimed Sonny, giving Angelo a fist bump. He looked into the rear-view mirror. "What d'ya say, Marianna?

Marianna swallowed hard. *It's now or never,* she thought. "Why not?" she said.

She could feel her pulse beginning to rise and a slight sweat accumulating under her arms.

"How do you want to play it, Marianna?" asked Sonny.

Marianna thought for a few moments. "How about I go in as a potential customer – assuming he's working today – and I begin to chat him up? You guys either come in a little later or just stand outside the window where I can point to you, letting him know I've got backup. And we'll see how that goes for openers. What d'ya think?"

Both Sonny and Angelo nodded their heads. "Sounds like a plan," said Angelo. "Perhaps you can convince Walter that it is in his best interest to come up with the cash. And if not, we come back at night and do a little more convincing."

"I think that there's a better way," said Marianna, causing both Angelo and Sonny to stare at her. "Before we rough him up, we want to get the money, right? The Elf wants his money and we want to teach him a lesson. So how about we let him know that we know where his kid is going to school and …"

"And that if he wants to keep her safe, he'd better deliver the cash," said Angelo, finishing her sentence.

"I like it," said Sonny, nodding, a big grin forming.

They parked the Escalade in the Porsche parking lot. It was about five o'clock. Like most dealerships, this one stayed open until about nine to catch the after-work and after-dinner crowd. Marianna freshened her lipstick, combed her hair, and unbuttoned the top button of her blouse. The guys gave her a thumbs-up. She sashayed into the showroom, smiling every step of the way; her eyes scanning for the tall, grey-haired fifty-something man with a slight beard as The Elf had described.

She began looking at a red 911 Cabriolet, running her fingers over the smooth surface. She reached out and put her hand on the door handle.

"Here, let me," said a baritone voice from behind her as he reached for the door. Marianna noticed the Rolex on his wrist. She turned and saw a silver-haired man in his fifties. His almost-white beard was close-cropped and neatly trimmed. His grey eyes sparkled. Walter Esterbrook opened the door of the 911, inviting Marianna to climb into the driver's seat. As she slid into the plush leather bucket seat, she allowed her skirt to rise to mid-thigh.

"My name is Walter Esterbrook," said the man. "Beautiful vehicle, isn't it?"

Esterbrook stood on the driver's side, bending down and peering inside the car at Marianna's exposed thighs, noticing the slight space between them.

"Very," said Marianna smiling. "Can you tell me something about the car and what makes it so special?"

Esterbrook walked around to the passenger side and slid into the seat. Marianna turned toward him, allowing her skirt to slide up another inch or two. Esterbrook noticed. *Definitely a player* thought Marianna. She knew exactly how she wanted to play this. She was, after all, an actress.

Esterbrook began explaining to her the difference between the Porsche and other sports cars, describing its balance, its history, and its cache: all the things that he thought would appeal to a young woman. "It's all class and no trash – but it is hot," he said, "much like yourself." He gave her a broad smile and a wink. Marianna returned the smile.

"Let me show you how to access the video control," said Esterbrook. "Everything can be controlled through the panel using the touch screen."

As he leaned forward, he rested his hand on the console, letting his fingers touch her exposed thigh.

"Do you like to play, Mr. Esterbrook?" asked Marianna, smiling coquettishly.

Esterbook turned his head away from the screen just slightly, continuing with his explanation of the car's features while allowing his hand to rest on her thigh. Marianna put her hand on top of his. His smile broadened.

"I think we have a playmate in common, Mr. Esterbrook," she said, beginning to squeeze his fingers. "His name is Elf."

Esterbrook froze and began to move away. Marianna used a wrist lock to keep him from leaving the car.

"Yes. My friend Elf says you like to play, but you don't like to pay," said Marianna, holding the wristlock and fixing him with her eyes.

Beads of sweat appeared on Esterbrook's brow. His smile disappeared. "Wha- what do you want?" he asked, his baritone voice quivering.

"We want twenty-five thousand dollars tonight. My friend Elf is getting impatient," she said.

"I don't have it," he exclaimed.

"Well, I suggest that you get it," she said, increasing the pressure on his wrist. "See those two gentlemen looking at that black Boxter?"

Esterbrook nodded, looking toward the car. Sonny and Angelo nodded in his direction.

"Well, they know where your sweet daughter goes to school," said Marianna, whispering in his ear. "And I am sure you wouldn't want anything to happen to her, would you?"

Esterbrook shook his head. He was perspiring profusely.

"We'll be back here at ten. Have the money, Mr. Esterbrook," said Marianna, giving his hand one final twist, causing his head to bang against the steering wheel. From the outside, it appeared as though he was showing her one of the car's many features.

Marianna let his hand go as she exited the vehicle. She smiled at him as he sat rubbing his wrist and hand. "Thank you for your thorough explanation," she said, loud enough for others to hear. "I want to bring my husband by to show him the car. I am sure he will love it as much as I do."

Marianna's heart was racing as she left the dealership and made her way back to the Escalade. *That went well.*

Angelo and Sonny caught up with her. "So what's the deal?" asked Sonny.

"I told him we'd be back at ten and that he'd better have the money," said Marianna. "I also told him we knew where his daughter went to school. That freaked him."

"Good job, cuz," said Angelo. "Ya know, whether or not he gets the cash, we're gonna have to teach him a lesson. We just can't have the word gettin' around that we're soft on crime." Angelo chortled. "That's a good one – soft on crime."

"Yeah," added Sonny. "And you're gonna have to teach him the lesson." He looked a Marianna with a raised brow.

"Now let's get something to eat," said Sonny. "I'm starved."

"You're always starved," said Angelo giving Sonny a shove.

Marianna wasn't thinking of food. She was thinking of ten o'clock. She tried to remind herself that this was just business and Walter Esterbrook was a sleazebag who deserved what he would get. But would she be able to do it? She knew that she could fight in self-defense or to protect someone else. She knew she could fight in anger, like in the nightclub. But would she be able to bust someone up because he was trying to default on a debt to a bookie? And what if he paid up? Could she hurt him just to teach him a lesson?

It reminded her of some parents who punish their child for stealing after the child has apologized and made restitution to the person he stole from. But then again, she thought, courts punish individuals who commit crimes even after the criminal makes restitution. *Restitution returns things to a previous state, but the behavior warrants punishment,* reasoned Marianna. The real question was whether she could be the one to issue the punishment. She also questioned whether corporal punishment was the best form of chastisement. Perhaps there was a better, less violent way.

These thoughts tumbled through Marianna's mind as the three cousins drove to a local deli for dinner. Angelo ordered a hot corned beef sandwich on rye with pickled tomatoes and a bottle of Heineken's. Sonny ordered a hot pastrami sandwich with French fries and a Bud. Marianna had a grilled vegetable sandwich with fries and a glass of iced tea. When Angelo and Sonny's sandwiches arrived, Marianna's eyes widened. Never had she seen so much meat stuffed between two slices of bread. The sandwiches had to be at least six inches high. She thought the three sandwiches were enough to feed a family of eight. Sonny noticed her look.

"What?" he asked. "They don't make corned beef sandwiches in LA?"

"Yeah, they do," replied Marianna, "but not gargantuan like that. Geez, they're humongous!"

Sonny smiled, picked up half the corned beef sandwich, opened his mouth wide, and shoved a corner of the sandwich in. His jowls expanded as though he had stuffed tennis balls into his cheeks. Some food fell back onto his plate. He took a slug of beer while he chewed. After the first bite, he smiled in satisfaction. Angelo followed suit. Marianna, on the other hand, took off the top slice of bread from her sandwich and divided the vegetables onto it, making two open-faced sandwiches. She took a small bite. She wasn't very hungry. All she could think about was what was coming later.

"So, what do you think is gonna happen?" asked Marianna.

Angelo wiped his mouth with the back of his hand and then used the napkin as an afterthought. "I think he's gonna come up with the money. They drive expensive cars, wear expensive watches, and live in high-end neighborhoods. They all bitch and moan, cryin' the I-ain't-got-no-money blues; but when push comes to shove, they always manage to find it."

"But I mean, after he gives us the money," replied Marianna. "What do we – uh – what do *I* do next? What do I do to him?"

"You could do what you saw us do in the alley," said Sonny. "Or you could come up with something different."

"Or you could break his legs," added Angelo. "We have a baseball bat in the van."

"Yeah, just like Ray Donovan," laughed Sonny as a bit of corned beef fell from his mouth. "Bam, one shot across the knee caps. That horse will never run again."

Marianna thought about that. "Isn't there a nonviolent way of issuing punishment?"

"Nah. We gotta deliver a message," said Sonny. "Not only to him but to anyone he knows who might even think about rippin' off one of our clients. These guys all know this is a dangerous business. Part of the draw is the risk. It gives them a hard-on. Same goes for guys who screw around on their old ladies. The risk of getting busted adds to the turn-on." Marianna knew he was right. She could feel herself becoming aroused.

"Of course, he'll whimper and beg us not to hurt him. But that's part of the game. I bet that a lot of these guys also get off on BDSM. A little bondage, a little dominance, a little sado-masochism… it all lights their fire. Think of the bragging rights this guy is gonna have, tellin' his buddies how he was roughed up by our hot little cousin." Both Sonny and Angelo laughed out loud. Marianna smiled, feeling more accepted by her male cousins.

But her stomach was churning as she thought about what was going to happen later that night. She didn't know whether she would be able to go through with it.

"You ain't gonna finish your sandwich?" asked Sonny, noticing that she barely ate anything.

"I'm not very hungry," replied Marianna, averting her eyes.

"We can have the waitress wrap it to go," said Sonny.

"How you feeling 'bout meeting Esterbrook?" asked Angelo, sensing her tension. "You ready to lose your cherry?"

It took a few moments for Marianna to catch his meaning. "I'm ready – sort of," she replied in a subdued voice just above a whisper. "I know you guys say it's just business, but still ..."

"I know what you mean, cuz," said Angelo. "You weren't raised in the streets. Your fighting was controlled in a gym. This is real. And this guy didn't do anything to you personally. I get it."

Marianna nodded her head, feeling comforted by her cousin's words of understanding.

"But if you're gonna be in *la famiglia*, ya gotta do it," continued Angelo. "You're gonna have to get used to it or fuggedaboutit. *Capisce?*"

"*Capisco,*" replied Marianna. "But what if I can't – I mean, tonight? What if I can't do it?"

Angelo looked at Marianna, then at Sonny, and back to Marianna. "One of us will take care of it. But you'll be out."

Marianna gave a quick nod and then lapsed into silence.

The waitress brought the check and took the remaining vegetable sandwich to bag it. After the bill was paid, the three of them got back in the Escalade. They had a couple of hours to kill before finishing their business.

They drove a few blocks away and parked the car on a secluded street near a dark alley. The one thing that was unique about New York and other vertical cities was that there were high-end luxury neighborhoods while just a block or two away there were homeless folks and drug deals being conducted. The Porsche dealer was in a posh area; but three short blocks away was another world. As long as everyone stayed where they belonged, there were no problems. Everyone had to respect the invisible boundaries.

Sonny and Angelo decided that the way they were going to proceed was to have Marianna meet Esterbrook by the dealership. She would meet him alone, not wanting to spook him. They figured she had already proven that she could handle herself. She would suggest they take a stroll away from the parking lot and the lights of the dealership to conduct their business. If anyone was watching, it would simply appear as though they were a couple on a walk. She would bring him to the alley. They decided that this approach was less risky than driving him somewhere and risk having the Escalade identified. The posh areas also had video cams all over; they didn't want to get caught on film.

At a few minutes before ten, Marianna put on her sunglasses and a baseball hat that Angelo handed her to keep the video cams from being able to identify her and began walking back to the dealership. She kept her head down. Angelo and Sonny were on the other side of the street, staying in the shadows while keeping an eye on her and the neighborhood. When Marianna got back to the dealership, she spotted Esterbrook leaning up against a Porsche Cayenne.

She walked up behind him and said, "Let's take a walk, Walter." She looped her hand into the crook of his arm and nudged him away from the lot. He felt her fingers squeeze the pressure points on the back of his forearm and recalled how she'd controlled him with the wristlock earlier. He didn't resist.

"Where are you taking me?" he asked, the beads of sweat re-appearing on his brow. "I brought you the money. Just take it and go," he implored.

"You want to get away from me, Walter," said Marianna. Her voice was throaty and sultry. "I thought you liked me. I thought you wanted me. Now you're in hurry to leave me." She pouted briefly.

Esterbrook's apprehension increased as they left the safety of the well-lit business district. Marianna could feel his body tense, and his pace slowed. She squeezed his arm; he winced. "Just another block," she said. "We'll have some privacy. I'll be all yours."

When they reached the alley, Angelo and Sonny grabbed Esterbrook and yanked him into the dark space. They had eliminated all the streetlights and relied just upon ambient lighting from the flickering neon signs. Their faces weren't visible.

"Okay, Walter," said Marianna, "now you can give me the present."

Walter Esterbrook reached into his jacket pocket and retrieved a fat envelope.

"It's all there," he said. "Twenty-five thousand, just like I promised. Now can I go? My wife – my family – is waiting for me." His voice shook as he spoke.

"Not quite yet, Walter," said Sonny. "Ya see, you made us go through a lot of work to track you down. The Elf tells us you kept making promises to pay, and he trusted you. But then, you go running off, forcing us to come find you. That's not a good thing."

Sonny kneed him in the groin, causing Esterbrook to double over in pain. He fell to his knees. Sonny looked at Marianna, signaling her with a quick movement of his head, indicating that it was her turn.

Marianna bent down, whispering in the gasping Esterbrook's ear.

"Ya see, Walter, crime doesn't pay," she said. "You can't make a business deal with someone and then walk away. And what would happen if others found out that there were no consequences for not fulfilling their obligations? What would happen to poor Elf's business? No, no, Walter. There must be consequences."

Angelo and Sonny were mesmerized by Marianna's performance. Little did they know that Marianna had put herself in a role from a script she had recently read. She was playing a part. And they were the audience.

Marianna ran her fingers through Esterbrook's hair, suddenly grabbing it tightly in her fist while pulling his head squarely into her rising knee with such force that they all heard the crack of his nose breaking. Esterbrook screamed.

"Shhhhh, Walter," said Marianna. "Just take your consequences like a man." She brought her leg into position and, using the heel of her foot, hooked Esterbrook in the back of his head. He fell face-forward onto the pavement, out like a light. The hook was one of the most powerful kicks in her repertoire. If executed correctly, it could be lethal.

Marianna looked at her cousins. "Enough?"

They nodded and the three of them walked away, leaving Esterbrook lying face down in the alley, his face bloody. He'd be out for a long while.

Marianna felt sick to her stomach. *Good thing I didn't eat that sandwich,* she thought.

CHAPTER FOURTEEN

Marianna was satisfied with being able to put herself in character and carry out her mission. Only this wasn't acting, and Walter Esterbrook's blood was real. She wanted to leave her options open with *la famiglia* and she didn't want to be seen as a loser by her new family. She knew, however, that she would have to live with the fact she'd committed a crime – a felony – she'd committed assault and battery on another human being. *Walter Esterbrook may have been a schmuck for getting involved with a street bookie, but he didn't deserve being beaten; at least not by me.* She had a conscience. She knew right from wrong. *Will I be able to separate my sense of morality and conscience from "it's just business," as Sonny and Angelo were able to do?* This was the sixty-four-thousand-dollar question. And even if she could, should she? *Acts of commission and acts of omission,* she thought.

She decided that she should give it a few more days before deciding. As expected, word of the events of the evening got back to the family. She received a lot of "atta-girls" from her cousins and from the rest of the family. Even Louie, she heard, seemed to be pleased with her performance. This was enough to keep her going, at least for a little while.

Marianna kept in touch with Grant mostly through texting; the three-hour time difference made texting the most convenient form of communication. Grant was not thrilled with her increasing involvement with her New York family. He knew better than to push back and Marianna was well-aware of his disapproval. She knew he missed her and she missed him. But she was obsessed. She just had to continue pushing forward.

Marianna went out on a few more assignments with Angelo and Sonny. Not all of them required that she beat someone up. Sometimes threats were enough. She often found that her acting skills were a great asset. She could act tough or seductive. Being female in the male-dominated world of the street could be made into an asset if she played her cards right. It threw people off their game, giving her an advantage. Much like in the martial arts, she would look for the vulnerability of her opponent rather than just go in to strike as hard as she could.

One of the strengths of the Mafia, she learned, was the number of connections it had with powerful people. Just as in most businesses, it wasn't what you know that mattered, it was *who* you know. *La cosa nostra* had a lot of connections. A lot of important people were beholden to the organization. Sometimes they gained their power through simple bribery. Even powerful people could be bought. When the price is right, people will sell their values to the highest bidder. Powerful people also could be threatened. Tell a politician that his family will be harmed unless he comes through with whatever is being requested, and weak politicians will cave. Many people in power (as is true of most people) have dark sides. The most righteous individuals and the most upstanding citizens have hidden secrets. If *la famiglia* could exploit these secrets, they could extract favors.

One evening, at the behest of Mike, Marianna, Sonny, and Angelo met for drinks to discuss a piece of business.

"Wassup, Pop?" asked Angelo after Mike had given everyone a hug and they'd ordered drinks.

"We gotta situation that I want you to fix," began Mike, looking from one face to the other. "And I think that you guys are the ones to take care of it. Especially you, Marianna."

Marianna was taken aback. She couldn't figure what she could bring to the table that her cousins couldn't do better. Both Angelo and Sonny stared at her and then back to Mike.

"One of our distributors got busted," continued Mike. "He was caught in a sting operation up in the Bronx and is lookin' at hard time in Rikers."

"I thought we had the DA on the payroll," said Sonny. "What's the problem?"

"That *is* the problem," replied Mike. "The Bronx DA, Gordon Blake, had a stroke and is in a coma. The Chief Assistant DA, Arthur Manning, is filling in until Blake recovers – if he recovers. Manning is a by-the-book, law and order kinda guy; and he's taking over. So, we gotta convince him that he should play ball with us."

"Why is this dude, who got busted, so important?" asked Angelo. "Let him do the time. He won't rat on us. And he'll survive in the joint."

"Nothin' is as easy as you would think," said Mike. "It seems that this guy is the son of one of your grandfather's goombas. And he's gay. He ain't gonna survive Rikers. Louie wants him out."

"And exactly how are we gonna do that, Pop?" asked Angelo. "That's beyond our pay grade."

Mike smiled. "Here's the thing," replied Mike. "Manning is married, with two young kids. He's a born-again type – but he has a secret, like a lot of those holier than thou guys. He likes the ladies." Mike turned toward Marianna, pointing his finger directly at her. "And that's where you come in."

Marianna just stared at her new uncle, not knowing what to say.

Mike continued. "He uses escort services, inviting the girls to a little apartment he has in Brooklyn. He likes his privacy. And from what we hear, he likes it rough – giving and receiving. I think he would like you. He likes petite ladies where he can be the big kahuna. Oh, and one more thing: he's black and he likes vanilla." Mike smiled.

Sonny looked at Marianna, who felt her face flush. "Hey, you'd be perfect for him," he said. "You're tiny, you're tough, and you're easy on the eyes, cuz. And you're white." He turned toward his uncle. "So, what d'ya wanna do?"

"As you know, we own a couple of escort services," replied Mike. "That's how we learned about his preferences. But it turns out that the guy plays too rough for many of our girls. No one wants to go out with him more than once. What we need to do is, the next time he calls for a 'date,' we send you, Marianna. Only this time you two guys are gonna go with her. We want to get pictures of him with Marianna. Pictures that we can use to convince Mr. Law and Order Born-Again DA that he wants to work with our family. You're an actress. You can play the part and you can take care of yourself. We all know that."

"How do you know that I'm his type?" asked Marianna. "I mean, how to know I will appeal to him?"

"We run a high-end service, catering to the special needs of our clients," began Mike. "We have a reputation for discretion which is why we have such a celebrated and diverse clientele. When a client is referred to us, we do a complete interview collecting as much detail as we can about the client's preferences. In the process, we learn a great deal about him. The interview is videotaped and we do a background check. We don't want to get ripped off and we want to protect our ladies against a bust or from harm. The girls also report back to us anything they learn from the johns. So, over time, we can build quite a file on the clients. And sometimes that file can be used to our advantage."

Marianna nodded in understanding. She was impressed with how everything was calculated.

"Do we know where the dude keeps his girly pad, Pop?" asked Angelo.

"Yeah. Why?" asked Mike.

"How about we go out there and set up our own sting?" said Angelo. "We can wire the place, have a video cam installed, and sit in a van taking all the pictures we want. If Marianna needs help, she can use a code world and bingo, we're there."

While Mike was thinking about Angelo's plan, Marianna was becoming more and more anxious. *Fuck, what have I gotten myself into? Fuck, my life was so simple. Now I gotta* ...

"Sounds good to me," said Mike. "We got all the connections. We got people who are good with surveillance and everything. Whatever you need. Just get it set up ASAP. You all right with that, Marianna?"

She knew this was important. It came directly from Louie. She couldn't say no.

"Uh, sure," said Marianna. "No problem." She knew that she didn't sound convincing, but no one said anything.

"All right, then," said Mike, finishing off his drink. "I'll leave the details to the three of you. Keep me posted on progress. Let me know when the place is wired and good to go. We're countin' on you." Mike stood up, smiled, and walked out.

"Shit," said Marianna. "We were just asked to set up a sting on the acting DA so that we can use him to get a drug dealer out of prison. And I'm being used as bait! What the fuck!"

"You wanted in, cuz," said Sonny. "This is your big shot. We pull this off and we get points, big time."

"And if we don't," replied Marianna, wide-eyed, "my ass is grass. I get banged, beat up, and potentially busted for trying to extort a DA. And we have no protection from City Hall!"

"We'll protect you and we'll make sure you're not hurt – or banged," added Angelo with a chortle. "We will be watchin'. We won't let anything happen to you, cuz."

Both Angelo and Sonny put their arms around Marianna and gave her a squeeze as they left the bar.

Over the course of the next several days, Angelo and Sonny were busy gaining access to the DA's *pied d'terre*. It wasn't that difficult. Dollar green works wonders in gaining access to places. The building superintendent was more than willing to look the other way when they were there. Sonny and Angelo's crew wore security system uniforms. If anyone asked, they were simply installing an updated system in the apartment. No one seemed to notice or care. Within a few hours, they were done. Later that night they sat in the van, testing the system for sound and video. It worked like a charm.

While they were setting things up, Marianna was working on developing a character for the most dangerous performance of her life. She knew that she would have to dissociate herself from the reality of what was going to take place. If she thought about it as a play or a movie, she could manage her anxiety. If she thought about the reality, she was afraid she wouldn't go through with it. Once she was in character, Marianna knew that even a big audience or a major audition wouldn't affect her. She became the character; she did not play to the audience. She would have to do the same with District Attorney Arthur Manning.

Marianna outlined a script for her performance. She developed the character in her mind. Now she had to come up with an appropriate wardrobe. She spoke with Sonny and Angelo about what she had in mind and asked them for a budget. If she was going to put herself on the line for this, she wanted to be prepared. Once she got their buy-in for what she had in mind, she set out on a shopping expedition.

She spent the better part of the day in Bloomingdales, outfitting herself. She also decided that on the day of operation, she would get her makeup done. She researched the internet to find a theatrical makeup salon. She wanted the makeup to fit the character while at the same time offering her some sort of disguise. Angelo had convinced her that Manning wouldn't press charges, regardless of how things went down. He wouldn't want the publicity. But Marianna was not about to take any chances. Marianna thought that

159

given Manning was a by-the-book, born-again kind of guy, he just might throw himself on the sword and turn her and himself in.

The day arrived. Marianna had gone to great lengths to prepare. Her bedroom was her dressing room. She stood in front of the mirror, touching up the makeup that had been meticulously applied earlier in the day. She put on her costume and waited.

The escort service called, telling Angelo that they'd received a confirmation from Manning. It was their custom to confirm with customers prior to sending out one of their escorts. At $1000 an evening, they didn't want to be going out for nothing. Despite their twenty-four-hour cancelation policy, they still experienced a no show every now and again. They also wanted to be able to book another client in the event of a last-minute cancelation.

Sonny knocked on the bedroom door, signaling it was time for them to get on the road. *Show time,* she thought.

Marianna walked out into the living room. She stood still for a moment, staring at her cousins. Sonny and Angelo just gawked. Marianna's dark hair was pulled severely back from her face in a tight pony tail. Her smoky eye shadow made her green eyes pop and accented her cheekbones. Her dangling ruby earrings matched her red lips. She wore a black, mid-calf, fitted Burberry raincoat with a belt that cinched tightly around her small waist. The red-soled, black Christian Louboutin stiletto heels added six inches to her height. The effect was exotic and intense, giving her both a sultry look and a 'don't fuck with me' appearance.

"What?" exclaimed Marianna. "Say something, for Christ sake!"

"Holy shit, Marianna, is that you?" exclaimed Angelo. "You look amazing! This guy is going to flip when he sees you."

Sonny continued to gape.

Marianna opened her Burberry, revealing a tight-fitting, Versace black, mid-thigh-length dress. She put one hand on her hip and gave both her cousins her best come-hither look.

"So you think I look okay?" she said as she lowered her head seductively.

Finally, Sonny found his words. "You look fan-fuckin-tastic!"

"Okay, then, let's do this!" said Marinna.

The three of them left the building and climbed into the Escalade.

"We set up a separate van near Author Manning's apartment," said Angelo. "Umberto's already watching just to make sure that everything goes according to plan, with no unexpected company waiting to share in the fun."

"Some fun," said Marianna, oozing sarcasm.

"Once we drop you off," continued Angelo, "we'll join Umberto in the van. We'll have eyes on you all the time, from the moment you leave us to the moment you reach Manning's apartment. There are cameras in both the living room and the bedroom. We even have a guy standing in front of the building to make sure you get up to the apartment without being followed. His name is Al. Don't talk to him; just go."

"If you feel you are in danger and want help right away," added Sonny, "just say 'I've gotta pee' or something like that. You chicks are always using the can."

Sonny and Angelo chuckled.

"Ha-ha," replied Marianna without a trace of humor.

Sonny pulled up in front of Manning's apartment building. It was a non-descript brick building built in the 1950s, complete with a front stoop and air-conditioners protruding from the windows. A tall, skinny guy wearing a hoodie was leaning against the railing, smoking a cigarette. Sonny flashed the car lights and the guy nodded. Marianna got out from the back of the Escalade. To anyone watching, it looked like she was being dropped off by Uber SUV. She walked past Al, giving him the slightest nod before reaching the intercom buttons used to announce her arrival. She located the one marked Unit 206, as she had been instructed, and pressed the button.

A baritone voice came through the speaker. "Yes."

"It's Angelina from the service," replied Marianna, whispering in a throaty voice.

Al smiled. The buzzer sounded and Marianna pushed open the door. Before it closed, Al ran up the four steps and stuck his foot out to prevent it from closing. He took out a piece of duct tape and covered the door lock so that it couldn't lock. Once he saw Marianna safely inside the elevator, he turned and nodded to Sonny who, with a slight squeal of tires, made a U-turn and parked near the surveillance van sitting around the corner. Both he and Angelo climbed into the van. The video monitor showed Marianna just exiting the elevator, slowly walking toward Unit 206.

She walked as though she were on camera both for her cousins' benefit and for DA Manning, whom she figured was peeking through the peephole in the door. No sooner had she reached the door than it opened. There stood Arthur Manning, an imposing figure looking more like a fashion model than a district attorney. He stood about six foot two, with brood shoulders and narrow hips wearing a loose-fitting tan cashmere sweater, brown linen slacks, and well-polished Gucci loafers without socks. He was a light-skinned African-American with a clean-shaven head, a single diamond stud in one ear, and a broad smile revealing perfect teeth. He was the epitome of urban sophistication.

"Hello, Mr. Manning. I'm Angelina," she said, extending her hand toward him.

"Welcome, Angelina. Please call me Arthur. And come in." He stepped back, still holding her hand, and made room for her to enter the apartment.

The next camera took over. Sonny and Angelo could see Manning and Marianna walking into the living room. *Angelina. Nice touch,* thought Angelo.

The apartment was a typical New York one-bedroom with a small kitchen barely big enough to accommodate one person plus the appliances. The living room was large enough to allow for a small dining table adjacent to the kitchen, a couple of stuffed chairs, a coffee table, and a three-person couch. End tables and lamps sat on either side of the couch. On one wall was a stocked bar with high-end brands of booze and a Bose sound system. Easy jazz played through the loudspeakers.

Marianna looked around, appraising her situation as well as admiring the man's impeccable taste in furnishings. It all spoke of class and urbane sophistication, much like the way he dressed.

Just as she was giving the apartment her once over, Manning was giving Marianna a once over as well. He smiled when he noticed her red-soled shoes.

"You like Christian Louboutin?" he asked with a smile.

163

"Indeed," replied Marianna, returning the smile. "And you're a fan of Mr. Gucci, I see."

They both chuckled.

"May I take your coat and offer you a drink?" Manning asked.

Marianna turned her back toward him and untied her coat belt, allowing him to help her out of her Burberry. She then turned toward him. "And I'll have a very dry martini, please. Grey Goose, if you have it."

Manning held her coat without moving as his eyes roved over Marianna's body from top to bottom, lingering for an extra moment at her cleavage, smiling all the while.

"Do you approve, Arthur?" asked Marianna, holding his eyes with hers and not smiling.

"Very much," said Manning, placing her coat in the closet near the front door before turning to the bar to prepare her drink. "Do you prefer olives or a twist, Angelina?" he asked as he poured the vodka into the silver martini shaker. He added several ice cubes and began to shake it.

"A twist, please," replied Marianna, taking a seat on the couch. She crossed her legs, allowing her skirt to rise on her thighs. Manning noticed.

He brought over two martinis, handing her one before sitting on the couch next to her. As she raised the glass to her lips, she felt his cool hand upon her bare thigh. It didn't move; nor did she. He took a sip from his glass, peering at her across the rim, watching for her reaction. She looked right back at him, holding his gaze.

Slowly, Manning placed his glass on the coffee table. He gently took hers out of her hand, placing it on the side table, and with one swift move he picked up Marianna and effortlessly carried her into the bedroom where he unceremoniously dropped her onto the king-size bed. He pulled his cashmere sweater over his head, revealing a perfectly sculpted chest and eight-pack abs. His smile turned to more of a smirk. He began to move, catlike, towards Marianna, as if stalking his prey.

Marianna decided to play along. She rose to her hands and knees, glaring at him as he circled the bed.

"I heard you like to play rough, Arthur," she hissed through her teeth.

Manning gave her a salacious smile, and his eyes sparkled. "Oh, yes," he said, nodding, his voice throaty.

"And do you like to talk dirty, Arthur?" asked Marianna, taunting him.

"Fuck, yes!" snarled Arthur. His nostrils flared.

"When are you going fuck me, nigga?" said Marianna, yanking her hair loose and letting it fall in front of her face. Her dress had already risen around her waist, revealing her thong. "You want some of this vanilla cooch?"

Manning kicked off his shoes and unbuckled his belt, allowing his pants to fall to the floor. He was not wearing underwear. His dark brown erection was as sculpted as the rest of his body. Marianna's eyes widened; she could feel herself becoming aroused in spite of herself. Manning climbed onto the bed and they circled each other.

"And you want some of this black cock, bitch. I can smell it."

Suddenly Manning lunged forward, reaching out to make a grab for Marianna's hair. She grabbed his wrist, flipping him onto his back, and quickly sat on his chest while jamming her forearm into his throat. *You are right, Arthur, I would love nothing more than to have you fuck me right now*, she thought. *But that's not gonna happen.*

"You are one mean, bitch, Angelina," said Manning through clenched teeth. "I'm gonna love giving it to you."

With that he gave a powerful buck, using both his legs and abdominals, tossing Marianna over his head. She was about to fall off the bed, but not before he caught her by the hair and hauled her back to the middle of the bed. He tore off her thong with one hand and pinned her with the other. He abruptly flipped her over onto her stomach, keeping one hand on the middle of her back, pinning her flat. He gave her exposed ass a smack, hard enough to leave his fingerprints. Marianna yelped. *Whoa, that felt good!*

"Sounds like you liked that," said Manning, grabbing her hair and raised his hand to give her another swat.

Marianna was afraid. She wasn't sure whether she was more afraid of being hurt or enjoying it. "Wait, Arthur ... I have to pee ... badly!" she yelled.

"Fuck!" said Arthur. "Now? Shit!" He rolled his eyes in exasperation. "Go ahead. But make it quick and get back so we can finish what you started, bitch."

Marianna jumped from the bed and ran to the bathroom, closing the door behind her. She sat on the toilet, panting. She knew her cousins would be there soon. Remember there was no video cam in the bathroom, she quickly plunged her fingers into her wetness and bit her lip to silence the moan. It didn't take long for her to climax.

Outside, she heard the apartment door slam open.

"What the fuck!" exclaimed Manning, too surprised to even cover himself.

Sonny and Angelo stood in front of Manning; one with a gun, the other a holding a baseball bat.

"Are you okay, Angelina?" yelled Angelo.

Marianna emerged from the bathroom. She had pulled down her dress and pulled back her hair. Her face was flushed. "Yeah, I'm fine," she said. She looked up at Manning. "I'm sorry, Arthur. This was fun; but business is business, ya know." She meant it.

Manning, recovered somewhat, sat down on the bed and pulled on his pants. "What the fuck is this all about, huh? Money? You want money?"

"Nah, Assistant DA Arthur Manning," began Angelo, "this ain't about money. It's about a favor."

"A favor? What kind of favor?" asked Manning, bending over to find his shoes.

"Ya see, you got a friend of ours in lock up," replied Angelo. "His name is Paulie D'Amato. He's in on a distribution charge. We want him out. Ya know what I'm sayin'?"

"Yeah, I know what you're saying," replied Manning, rubbing his bald palate. "And if I don't do you this favor?"

Sonny scratched the side of his cheek. "We don't think you would want us to show the videos of you and, uh, Angelina, playing games in this secret hideaway to your wife and kids – or to your pastor." Sonny glared at Manning with a wry grin.

Manning glared back. His face contorted in a venomous sneer. He then turned toward Marianna and hissed, "You fucking bitch!"

Marianna shrugged.

Manning's shoulders sagged. He held his head in his hands, not moving. After a few moments, he picked up his sweater from the floor, put it on, and stood up, inserting his feet into his Guccis. He had regained his composure. "Fun and games are over," he said calmly. "How's this gonna play out?"

Angelo stepped forward. "First, you are going drop all charges against Paulie D'Amato," he said. "Once he's released, you go about your business as always."

"And what about the tapes?" asked Manning.

"Let's say we'll keep them in a safe place," replied Angelo. "You, DA Manning, and my family are now partners. Ya never know when we might need another favor."

Manning nodded. He knew the rules. It was now a new ballgame. "And what do I get out of this?"

Angelo paused for a moment. He looked at Marianna and then back at Manning. "First, Your Pleasure Escort Service won't charge you for the fun you had with our cousin," said Angelo. A broad smile spread across his face. "And second, ya never know when you may need a favor from us. The favors go both ways. We're partners, remember?"

Manning understood life as he knew it was over. It was a whole new ballgame. He was now in bed with the mafia.

And with that, the three cousins turned and walked out of the apartment, leaving a somewhat dazed Manning behind. As they left the building, Al, who had been on lookout, joined them as they walked to the van. Sonny gave him a thumbs-up and Al got inside. The cousins crossed the street, climbed into the Escalade, and drove off. All in a night's work.

Poor bastard, thought Marianna as she was lying in bed later that night thinking about what happened. *Like the rest of us, Mr. Law and Order, born again family man DA Arthur Manning, has a dark side. He doesn't hurt anyone. But he got busted. Now his life will be forever changed.* With that thought in mind, she fell asleep.

CHAPTER FIFTEEN

Mike and the rest of the family, especially Louie, were very pleased with Marianna. Angelo and Sonny had filled them in on what had gone down with DA Arthur Manning. They were impressed with her moxi. She had guts and courage; she put herself on the line for *la famiglia.* Such fealty was of paramount importance to Louie. Family and loyalty were of supreme value for the entire mafia organization. And violations were treated harshly. Marianna had garnered high marks for her performance. And it meant more to her than winning an Oscar.

But at the same time, it added to an internal conflict. She agonized over which direction she was going to go. She knew that her husband would not want any part of the syndicate, and he would be adamantly opposed to doing anything illegal. If she were going to become part of her other family, she would have to leave him and everything they'd built together. She surprised herself, that she was even considering such a move. Had she been given the choice as a hypothetical question prior to her visit to New York, she would have been certain that there was not even a remote possibility of making that change.

She also struggled with whether she was really capable of living this life on a fulltime basis. She thought about what was going to happen to Arthur Manning. He'd given into his dark side, and there would be no turning back the clock. *You can't put toothpaste back in a tube.* Marianna even wondered how she would live with what she had already done, not to mention how she would live with the things she would be expected to do if she joined the family.

She was already deeply troubled by what she had seen and done. She still hadn't recovered from the image of Sonny severing the gangbanger's finger with the garden shears. The thought that she'd smashed Walter Esterbrook's nose for no reason other than to prove herself to Louie left her nauseous. And then there was Arthur Manning. Not only did she feel badly for him, but she felt guilty for becoming sexually aroused by the confrontation. *I would have fucked him,* she thought. If it wasn't for the cameras and cousins watching, she might have. And this bothered her. She didn't know who she would become – who she had already become.

She knew that Angelo and Sonny had to separate from their emotions and their morality in order to function in the organization. She knew they were not inherently bad people. They were not psychopaths. They'd simply grown up in a family where there were two sets of values – those that were sanctioned by the larger society in which they lived and those that were expected in the sub-culture that was their family and *la cosa nostra*. They'd had to dissociate themselves from people who were not a part of the organization. They had to keep their personal world secret from others who were not part of *la cosa nostra*. They'd learned the art of subterfuge when with outsiders.

Marianna wasn't sure that this is what she wanted for herself. Like Walter White in *Breaking Bad,* she feared that her dark side might take over and become the dominant aspect of her personality.

Marianna remained in New York for an additional ten days, but then it was time to bid the family goodbye. Grant was becoming impatient. And she needed time to process everything that had happened. She knew she wouldn't be able to process anything while embedded in the family. There was a goodbye dinner at Lena and Vinnie's home that Sunday. Marianna would leave for LA late that afternoon. She packed her roller-board, suitcase, and backpack, and with Sonny's help, placed them in the back of the Escalade, and, together with Sonny and Angelo, drove to Lena and Vinnie's place. The entire family was present, all twelve of them, including Grandpa Louie. Everyone wanted to say goodbye.

Once again, Marianna sat to Louie's left and Angelo sat across from her. This time Vinnie, as the host, sat at the other end of the table. Everyone expressed their good wishes and how happy they were to have met Marianna and how much they looked forward to having her in the family. The younger members of the family all indicated that they intended to keep in touch with her, and would tweet her, Facetime with her, and even Instagram. It made Marianna smile.

Louie leaned toward her.

"You did good, *la mia bella nipote*," he said with a smile. "But before you decide to move here permanently, I want you to go home and think about it. Take as much time as you need. There will always be a place at the table for you here." He then leaned toward her and whispered, "You will always be part of the family even if you choose not to be part of *la famiglia*."

Everyone nodded and raised their glasses in agreement. In unison, they all shouted, "Cin cin!"

Vinnie added. "And even if you decide that you don't want to move to the Big Apple, there will always be a place at our table whenever you're in town."

Again, they all raised their glasses nodding in approval. Marianna felt the love. Her eyes welled up.

"Hey," said Sonny from down the table, "bad-assed broads like you don't cry, cuz!" Everyone laughed.

"I heard that Mr. Manning wants to see you one more time before you go," said Angelo with a devilish grin.

"Yeah, and he wants a copy of the video for his collection," added Sonny with a smirk. "He'll pay top dollar."

Marianna turned beet red. The younger children didn't know what was going on.

"What video?" asked Junior. "I wanna see."

"Me, too," said Carla.

"Now look what you've gone and done," said Lena, giving them a scowl.

"We're just yanking her chain, Ma," said Angelo.

"Well, just stop; and I mean now!" replied Lena. But she couldn't help grinning.

"Sorry, cuz," said Sonny. "The tapes are all locked up in a vault that nobody can get to. Not even us."

"And there are no copies," reassured Angelo.

It just occurred to her that the entire family, except for the younger ones, had probably seen the tape of her crawling around on the bed with Manning. She was mortified. No one noticed. They all chatted amiably, joking, teasing, wishing her well, and, of course, eating. To them, business was business, and everyone did what they had to do. This was *la famiglia*.

When it was time to leave, there were hugs from everyone. One by one, they wished her well and indicated that they looked forward to seeing her again. Grandpa Louie gave her a kiss on both cheeks and sent her on her way.

As soon as they got into the Escalade, Marianna said, "You bastards better never show that tape to anyone – or get off on watching it yourselves, you pervs!"

"But you're so damned hot, cuz," said Angelo, laughing.

Marianna smacked him on the back of his head. She couldn't help but smile.

They dropped her off in front of American Airlines, giving her a final hug goodbye. Marianna had two hours before her plane was to leave. She spent the time making phone calls.

Her first call was to Grant. She told him that she missed him and could hardly wait to see him. They chatted about things in general; Grant gave her an update on the animals and the latest stuff about the house, and things in general. They both knew that a detailed conversation would take place when she was home.

She then called Tony. She told him that she had met with the entire family and thought they were great. She also told him that his siblings all sent him their love and wanted him to know they missed him. When she told him that she was considering moving to New York to become part of the family, he became outraged. He was furious with his father for introducing Marianna to the business.

Tony understood Louie all too well. He knew that Louie had little interest in Marianna, but was using her to get to him. He also knew that once Marianna was exposed to the business, Louie would not simply leave her alone. She knew far too much about the business, and that could be used against the family. Marianna did not tell him about the sting operation. She had her own misgivings about the tape being out there. The last thing she needed was to hear a diatribe from Tony.

Her next call was to her parents. When she told her parents that she was considering relocating, her mother cried. Her father, on the other hand, became enraged. He unleashed all the pent-up rage he had suppressed toward Tony, first for abandoning Mary when she got pregnant, and then for introducing Marianna to Louie. Marianna was completely caught by surprise; she had never seen her father so out of control. She had assumed her parents would be upset about her even thinking about moving to New York, but she hadn't expected the outpouring of rage from her father. Only once before had she seen him so angry. She had long ago repressed this memory. Now she remembered. She realized that this was what got triggered when Tony unexpectedly blew up at her when she didn't want to visit him.

She had just graduated from high school and was in love with a boy a few years older. The boy was attending college in the Midwest somewhere and was visiting his grandparents in her city. Marianna had met him at a party and had given him her phone number. When she'd told her parents that she wanted to go out with him, Victor exploded and told her that if she went out with him, she would have to leave his house. In effect, he'd threatened to kick her out on her own. She'd never understood why he had become so enraged. She now knew that he must have been reliving his experience with Mary and Tony and hadn't wanted the same thing to happen to her.

Here he was again, exploding. And a lot of it was directed toward her for even wanting to associate with Louie, the man who'd threatened to take her away from them and who had covered up Tony's felonious behavior. Marianna was totally unprepared for the onslaught. It brought her to tears. She had never thought just how profoundly her decision might affect her parents, other than they would miss having her located near them on the West Coast. It was one thing for her to want to meet with her birth father, but an entirely different thing to want to become a part of the family whose memory they were trying to expunge from their lives. That was one thing she hadn't thought about. *So much for being sensitive to the feelings of others,* she thought.

Marianna could handle Tony's anger; she even expected it. He had done it before. But her parents were a totally different thing. She didn't want to hurt them and she certainly didn't want to alienate them or have them angry at her.

She also understood why it felt like she walked on eggshells around men - even Grant. She never could figure out why or when they would erupt for no apparent reason. Her early experience with her father had made an indelible imprint on her and had left her wary.

Marianna both dreaded and looked forward to discussing the entire situation with Grant, her go-to person.

She knew that talking with her husband was going to be difficult, which was why she wanted to wait to have the major part of the conversation in person. But now, after hearing her parents' reaction, she was even more concerned about how Grant would respond. She felt confused and alone. It was going to be a long six-hour flight. She feared the conversation that awaited her and felt comforted by the fact that she would have time to think. She only wished that she had someone to talk with about her decision. She needed to talk it through with someone who had no vested interest in the outcome.

The public-address system announced that her plane was ready for boarding. She passed through the ticket checker and moseyed down the jet bridge into the plane. As she wandered down the aisle, her mind swirled. She felt confused; almost disoriented. She located her seat, placed her roller board in the overhead storage area, climbed over the passenger occupying the aisle seat, and plopped herself down next to the window. She closed her eyes and was on the verge of tears. She forced herself to breathe slowly and evenly. She fell into a deep sleep.

Out of the corner of her eye she noticed the passenger sitting next to her. He looked familiar.

"Dr. Sherman?" she inquired, recognizing the face.

The man turned toward her. "Marianna!" he exclaimed with a broad smile. "How nice to see you. How are you?" His eyes twinkled when he smiled, giving her a warm feeling.

"Uh, um, I'm doin' alright," she lied. "What are you doing here?" Marianna realized that it was an inane question, but that was the best she could do.

"I'm just returning to LA from a conference in New York," he replied. "And you?"

She hesitated. "I'm, uh, I was visiting family."

"I hope it was fun," said Dr. Sherman. "It's so nice to see you. One of the sad parts of being in my profession is that, when patients finish their work in therapy, I often never hear from them again. I never find out how they're doing after the work is done. How are you really doing Marianna?" His tone was sincere. That was one of the things she'd liked most about

177

her former psychotherapist: the sound of his voice. She remembered that she often would call his voicemail just to hear his voice; she'd found it comforting.

Marianna looked into Dr. Harold Sherman's gentle eyes. He was the only person with whom she felt totally comfortable sharing her most private thoughts and with whom she felt comfortable being totally vulnerable. She cherished the years she'd spent as his patient before marrying Grant. If it weren't for him, she thought, I never would have married Grant, and who knows where I would be today. His soft voice, gentle eyes, and genuine concern for her wellbeing had been as palpable then as it was now. She felt the tears fill her eyes and spill over, running down her cheeks.

"Oh, Dr. Sherman," she whispered, "I am a mess. Everything was going great until a few weeks ago. And now…" She interrupted herself allowing the tears to flow. Dr. Sherman said nothing, maintaining an emotional connection while at the same time giving her the space she needed.

When her crying subsided, Marianna said: "It's really a miracle that you should happen to be on this plane at this time. Just before boarding, I was thinking I could use someone to talk to right now; and, poof, here you are, like a genie materializing from a bottle." She paused, a slight smile creeping through her tears. "As much as I would love a session right here, right now, I do not want to take advantage of you or intrude on your time. But if you would, if you could – I would pay you…"

"Don't worry about it, Marianna," said Dr. Sherman with a warm smile. "I have nowhere to go and nothing else to do. So why you don't just tell me your story and we'll see what happens."

"Are you sure? I mean –" she began, feeling both a desire to spill her guts and a reserve about not wanting to take advantage of her old therapist.

Dr. Sherman nodded, and speaking in his soft, understanding way, he said, "I'm sure. Just start at the beginning and tell me what happened during the last few weeks to put you in such a state."

In hushed tones, so as not to be overheard by other passengers, Marianna began telling Dr. Sherman her story. She told him everything, from the time she'd met Tony to the present, including her meeting Louie and the things she'd done while in New York. She left nothing out. She knew that everything she said would be held in the strictest confidence, not only because Dr. Sherman was governed by the patient-doctor privilege, but because that was the type of man he was. She felt a huge sense of relief just getting it all out on the table. Dr. Sherman listened attentively.

"That's one incredible story, Marianna," he said. "You start off just wanting to meet your biological father and end up meeting an entire mafia family that you didn't know you had."

"If I hadn't lived it, I would think it sounded like a movie script," said Marianna with a sardonic smile.

"Truth often is stranger than fiction," responded Dr. Sherman grinning.

"So what should I do, Dr. Sherman?" pleaded Marianna. "I'm so confused. I have to admit that it was very exciting knowing that I was living on the edge, living life by a different set of rules. But it runs so counter to everything I believe – or thought I believed. And to who I thought I was."

179

Dr. Sherman thought for a moment. "Yes, I suppose it would be exciting, as long you don't get caught."

She knew he wasn't judging her; just stating the facts.

"Yeah, I suppose that's true," she said thoughtfully. "I really didn't give that much thought."

"Just as you didn't think about how your parents would react," he said in a matter of fact tone.

"I wonder what other consequences I didn't think about," murmured Marianna, more to herself than to Dr. Sherman. She looked out of the window, watching the clouds. "I suppose Grant might want a divorce. He might end up hating me, just like my father does."

"I don't think your father hates you, Marianna," said Dr. Sherman. "He is more hurt and frightened, not to mention unleashing stored-up anger from the past."

Marianna raised her eyebrows. "Why would he be frightened?"

"Frightened for what could happen to you," began Dr. Sherman. "Fathers are protective – they're hard-wired that way. And perhaps frightened that Louie might once again become involved in his and your mother's lives in some way. Remember, fear for your safety is what prompted them to take the deal from Louie in the first place."

Marianna nodded. It's amazing how much Dr. Sherman remembered, she thought. She sat quietly, reflecting upon what Sherman had said about her father's fears. That was something else she hadn't thought about.

"I wonder if this entire experience was more of a message than a suggestion that you make a permanent decision," said Dr. Sherman.

"How do you mean, a message?" asked Marianna. Her brow raised.

"Well, it's like a dream," replied Dr. Sherman. "Remember how we used to interpret dreams as messages from our unconscious? Perhaps this is a message telling you that you need to honor your dark side and make some changes in your life."

"My dark side?" Marianna's eyebrows knitted in puzzlement.

"Each of us has a dark and a light side to our personality," explained the doctor. "Just as all of us have a male and female part of our personality –"

"The animus and anima," interjected Marianna, remembering their conversations about the work of Carl Jung. "Male and female parts to our makeup."

"Yes," acknowledged Dr. Sherman. "Human beings are filled with dualities. We all have good and bad and light and dark in our personality, as well; like devils and angels. Most people have more light than dark, and more good than bad. And for some, it's the other way around. So even in the worst of us, there is some good and –"

"There's bad even in the best of us, right?"

"That's right," said Dr. Sherman. "But the thing is that most of us don't want to honor the bad. We don't even want to acknowledge that it exists. We try to push it into our unconscious. Maybe instead we have to find a balance between the two."

"So you're suggesting that this experience I had in New York with my mafia family may have given expression to my dark side, but that I don't have to live it?" asked Marianna, sensing some sense of relief at the thought.

181

"Maybe you need to find some sense of excitement in your life that gives vent to that part of your personality," suggested Dr. Sherman. *"You described your life as satisfying and fulfilling, but you didn't mention anything that suggested adventure or excitement."*

"I suppose my life is kinda dull. And maybe if I had more adventure in my life, I wouldn't have been as attracted to this other life?" asked Marianna. *"Do you think that's why I am so attracted to these TV shows that portray characters with dark sides?"*

Dr. Sherman smiled. *"What do you think?"*

"Yeah, maybe," said Marianna, nodding her head. *"I sorta live vicariously through them. And I love getting acting roles where I can be a bit naughty or evil."*

"Acting is a great way to give expression to that part of who you are," agreed Dr. Sherman. *"And didn't you act out a bit while in high school and after your bout with cancer?"*

His memory is amazing! *"Yeah, but I put all that stuff behind me. I saw where it might lead,"* replied Marianna.

Dr. Sherman nodded with a smile. *"Right. You were concerned with consequences."* He paused for a moment. *"Weren't you a martial artist?"*

"Yeah. Good memory, doc," said Marianna. *"But I stopped competing a while back. Maybe I should compete again. I could kick some serious butt."* She laughed.

"I bet you could, Marianna, I bet you could," said Dr. Sherman with a broad smile and twinkling eyes.

Marianna looked at him for a long moment. *"Thanks, Dr. Sherman. Thanks for listening. As always."*

"You're welcome," replied Dr. Sherman. *"Now I think I am going to take a nap."*

"And I am going think about all we said," replied Marianna, reclining her seat and closing her eyes.

The public-address system squawked, startling Marianna awake. She looked toward the passenger on her left; she was a grey-haired middle-aged woman. The flight attendant announced their arrival at LAX. Marianna smiled as she realized she had been dreaming an imaginary session with her former therapist. She understood that dreams can be wish-fulfillment as well as messages from the unconscious to the conscious. She would give the dream careful consideration. She also knew that she would definitely make an appointment to see him, the sooner the better.

All the way to LA, she puzzled over her decision. She weighed the pros and cons. She thought about everything she and Dr. Sherman had talked about in her dream, especially the part about the dark and light side of her personality. She also thought about her father's anger and hurt. She certainly did not want to put her parents in jeopardy. Being so caught up in the excitement, until today, she hadn't thought about the consequences if she was busted. Nor did she think about the consequences to herself of having to live with the memories of the things she did. She also realized that none of her other family ever discussed getting caught; it was not part of their thinking. *Jeez, and here I thought I was methodical, deliberate, and even forensic in my thinking. How could I not have thought about all of these potential consequences? I guess it's similar to gymnastics or the martial arts. If you thought about getting hurt you'd never do it or at least you wouldn't do it well.*

She questioned her morality. As exciting as it had been to be involved in adventures with Sonny and Angelo, could she actually see herself going against everything she had believed in and everything she stood for? On the other hand, she feared losing contact with her New York family. It was true that they all wanted her to be part of the family. But, in reality, would she have to sacrifice her values or sacrifice *her other family*? She realized that twenty years ago, this had been *bio-dad*'s dilemma as well. In his case, and at that time, it was an all or nothing proposition. He was cut off from the family for the decision he made. Would that happen to her? She remembered both Vinnie and Louie saying that no matter what decision she made, she would always be welcome at the family table.

Had I been pumped on adrenalin? Was I addicted to the rush? Would I be willing to sacrifice everything? How important is my other family? More important than my birth family? More important than my husband? Am I willing to put everything at risk?

When the plane landed, she knew what she had to do.

CHAPTER SIXTEEN

G rant was at the airport to meet her. He stood at the bottom of the escalator, holding a bouquet of flowers. As soon as Marianna saw him, she felt a warm rush. His smiling, unshaven face filled her heart. Right then and there his presence confirmed the direction in which she had been leaning: she was not going to become an active member of *la famiglia*. She was going to remain where she felt she belonged.

Marianna rushed into the outstretched arms of her husband. Tears rolled down her face; tears of pure happiness.

Grant whispered in her ear. "I am so glad you're back."

She pulled away enough to look up at him with tear-stained cheeks. "Yes, I am back. Really back," she said with a warm smile.

Grant looked at her, puzzled, but said nothing. He took her backpack and slung it over his shoulder. With one hand, he pulled her suitcase and he held Marianna's hand with the other as she pulled the roller-board. She buried her nose into the bouquet and breathed in the perfumed aroma of the flowers as they walked to the parking lot. Grant placed the luggage in the back of the Jeep and he and Marianna climbed into the front seats; but before they left the parking spot, Marianna gave him a long, passionate kiss, placing her hand on his crotch and squeezing. Grant murmured. His face filled with a look of surprise.

Without losing a beat, he reclined the seat. Marianna's lips were glued to his as she released his engorged cock, hoisted her skirt above her hips, moved her thong aside, and guided him into her wetness. She began to grind as Grant began his slow thrusts, penetrating deep inside her. It didn't take long before desire, longing, and absence brought them to climax. Grant smiled. "I guess you missed me, too," he said catching his breath.

"Ya think?" Marianna replied. *Hey, Dr. Sherman, is that naughty enough for you?* she thought, smiling.

As they drove home from LAX, Marianna filled Grant in on what had happened while she was in New York - at least, most of it. She told him about some of her adventures and her meeting the various members of her other family. She indicated that she intended to keep in touch with them, but had no intention of moving to New York. Grant expressed some concern about Louie and the code of loyalty. Just like her father, he worried whether, now that Marianna knew about the family business, would Louie leave her alone? And now that Grant knew some of what they are doing, would he be in danger as well? *What have I done?* she thought. *Have I put all those whom I love in danger? OMG!*

"I think I'll wait a few days before calling Louie to tell him what I've decided," said Marianna. "I want to let things settle down – for me and for him. I also want to talk with my parents again. They were pretty upset the last time I spoke with them."

"Yeah, I know," said Grant, looking straight ahead as he drove them home.

"You know?" asked Marianna, turning toward him, her eyes flashing.

"What d'ya think?" replied Grant, his voice stoic. "Did you think that you could just tell your mother and father that you were planning to stay in New York and become part of a mafia family, and they wouldn't call me?"

Once again Marianna was taken aback by her own lack of prescience. She'd never thought of herself as lacking judgment or the ability to foresee the consequences of her decisions. But here it was again. She hadn't given it a thought. She was so wrapped up in her own world that she'd completely lost sight of the unintended consequences of her actions.

She felt contrite. "So why weren't you furious?" she asked, filled with chagrin. "Why the flowers?"

"Simple. I love you," said Grant, keeping his eyes straight in front of him. "I'm not stupid. I kinda figured that you might have gotten swept away by the thrill of being involved in a real-life *Sopranos* drama; your own realty show. I was hoping that once the adrenalin left your system, you would return to being your customary, rational self."

Marianna felt a smile cross her lips. "I guess," she said. "But I still have to deal with my mess." *It was that totally rational me that got me into this mess to begin with. Rational my ass! That's got to change.*

Grant filled in Marianna about what her parents had told him. He explained that her father had told him about his outburst and how he regretted it.

"He didn't mean to unload all over you," said Grant. "It was just that so much had been suppressed for so many years."

"I get that," replied Marianna. "I'm just glad to hear that he is not still angry at me. It will make talking with them a lot easier."

"There will be time enough for that tomorrow," said Grant. "Once we get home, it will be time for you to get a good night's sleep. Call them in the morning."

Marianna nodded. "You're so wise, my love. When did that happen?"

"It comes with grey hair," replied Grant, chuckling.

"So what's been happening here aside from my drama?"

Grant smiled. "Same old, same old. Just the same uneventful, boring life you left behind." He proceeded to fill her in on the latest news: the dogs, the goings-on.

"I love our life... and it's not boring." She gave him an impish smile, touching his inner thigh. "But I do intend to spice it up a bit. You game?"

Grant grinned as he drove into their driveway. The dogs raced over to Marianna, licking her in excitement and not even waiting until she was completely out of the Jeep.

What was I thinking! she thought as she scratched and petted the excited animals.

The next morning, she called her parents. They both expressed great relief upon hearing that Marianna had arrived home safely and, more importantly, that she was going to remain home. Marianna apologized for frightening them and for potentially putting them in harm's way. She especially apologized to her father, who was quick to apologize to her for his outburst. He said he had to admit that it felt good to let it out after so many years, but regretted putting her in the eye of the storm.

"Sometimes it's necessary to express that dark side, Dad," said Marianna. "It's not something we Boltons are good at, ya know. We keep secrets and store things up until the lid blows."

"I suppose you're right, my lovely daughter," replied her father. "Maybe we should become more Italian."

They both laughed. Marianna was very much relieved when she hung up the phone.

Marianna spent the next several days catching up on all the things she'd neglected while she was away. She called up the martial arts studio where she had previously trained and talked with her instructor. He was delighted to hear that she wanted to resume training and begin competing again. She also scheduled an appointment to see Dr. Sherman. His next available time was two weeks away. She also called her agent, telling her that she wanted to audition for darker shows where there was a strong female protagonist; ones with a dark side, where the women were dealing with their own inner demons. She felt good taking actions that would jumpstart her life.

One day, while she was in the midst of reading a script, she received a text from her cousin Angelo, saying, "Tony's here."

CHAPTER SEVENTEEN

Marianna immediately booted up her computer and opened Facetime. She had to chat with Angelo. He was quick to respond.

"What's going on, Angelo?" asked Marianna.

"Hey, Marianna. How're ya doin'?" replied Angelo as though nothing was going on.

"Never mind me; what's this about Tony being in New York?" Marianna was more than just curious. She felt apprehensive.

"Well, it seems that once Tony learned that you were going to go into the family business, he called Louie," replied her cousin.

"Why the fuck would he do that?" She felt her pulse rate jump.

"I'm not sure exactly," said Angelo. "But the way it came down to me is that Tony didn't want you in the business. He was so angry about Louie even considering letting you come in that he was willing to make a deal with Louie."

"A deal? What kind of deal?" Marianna felt her apprehension turn to agitation. A deal with Louie was like making a deal with the devil.

"Tony wanted to take your place," replied Angelo. "He would take over. He'd move back to New York and become part of the family. How about that!"

"You've got to be fuckin' kidding me!" exclaimed an irate Marianna.

"Nope. That's the way it went down. It seems –" Angelo hesitated. He looked away.

"What? It seems what?" Marianna could barely sit still.

"Uh, well, it seems that's what Louie wanted all along," said Angelo, his voice low and somber. "He wanted Tony back. And he was using you to get to Tony."

Marianna froze. Angelo continued.

"The deal is: Tony agreed to come back into *la famiglia* providing that Louie cut you loose and left you and your parents alone. As long as Louie stayed away from you and your parents, Tony would take over when Louie died. The family all got together for a meeting. There was lots of yelling and arguing, but at the end of the day the *capo* Louie prevailed. Tony's in, you're out. *Finito*. I'm sorry, cuz, but business is business."

It all made sense. Tony had been right all along. Louie had been playing him. His father hadn't lost his touch. Even at eighty, Louie was still the conniving, manipulative crime boss. Don Louie Donatello. *Old guys rule,* thought Tony.

This was the only way Tony could redeem himself as a father and from his nefarious, irresponsible past – he could protect his daughter from his father's influence. He could keep her safe. He could redeem himself, at least in his own eyes, for all those years of having taken advantage of her mother and others by hiding behind the shield of his father's connections and power. He could finally be the father he never was; he could be the protector he was supposed to be.

Marianna's face was burning. She felt a mixture of hurt, sadness, anger, relief, and strangely, love. Tony, her *bio-dad,* had sacrificed his life for her. He was willing to put his own marriage and family on the line for her.

"Are Tony's wife and daughter with him in New York?" asked Marianna.

Angelo shook his head. "His wife hasn't made up her mind and his daughter is gonna stay in San Francisco," replied Angelo. "She likes her job."

Marianna looked at Angelo, who just sat quietly, waiting.

"Hey, Angelo," she said barely above a whisper, "What about us? Does that mean that you and I, Sonny, the whole family - can't be family? I mean ..."

"No. Of course not. But it *does* mean that you'll have to forget everything you know, heard, saw, or, if possible, did. Like it never happened. Make it disappear from your mind. And we can never talk about it, and you can't ask questions. The only thing we can do is shoot the shit, you know, like normal people. No business. *Capisce?*" Angelo chuckled.

"*Io capisco,*" she replied.

"Hey, cuz, I gotta go," said Angelo. "There's some business I gotta take care of."

"I hear ya, cuz. Thanks for the heads up. See ya!"

Angelo smiled and clicked off.

Marianna sat quietly, trying to collect her thoughts. After several minutes, she smiled. She was looking forward to telling both her parents and Grant the latest developments.

***

A few months later the Marianna-Tony episode of the documentary aired on national television. Her smartphone began to chirp with texts and emails pouring in from friends and relatives. Among them were several from Angelo, Sonny, and the rest of her other family in New York.

ACKNOWLEDGEMENTS

It is my pleasure to acknowledge Joanna Fiore whose contributions to all aspects of this story cannot be over-estimated. She has been an inspiration and a friend, as well as a kick-ass physical trainer. I am thankful for connecting with my editor, Carol Wallis, whose eagle-eye, alacrity, and dedication to her craft has contributed to making this a far better book. And lastly, I want to express appreciation to my wife, Barbara, for her patients and she listened to me endlessly taking through various sections of this manuscript and the development of the characters.

ABOUT THE AUTHOR

After having written five nonfiction books, when I turned 75 when I decided to turn my attention to writing psychological fiction. During my fifty-plus years as a practicing psychologist, I have been privileged to enter the lives of countless people as their psychotherapist. Their lives and conflicts revealed profound truths about the human condition. Their stories and their struggles inspired me. Many of their stories and their struggles have provided themes for my books. Sometimes a common issue, rather than a specific individual, stimulated the stories. More than once, their stories resonated with my own life and helped me to gain clarity and perspective. I am profoundly grateful for the insights provided by those who entrusted me with their stories and permitted me to join them on their journey of self-discovery.

I was born and raised in The Bronx in New York City, lived in a five-story walk up apartment with my parents and younger sister, attended City College of New York earning both a bachelor's and master's degree, and a Ph.D. in Clinical Psychology from the University of Kansas.

I am now semi-retired from clinical practice and devote the rest of my time to writing, cooking, woodworking, photography, and exercise.

I have been married to my wife, Barbara, for over thirty years, have three grown children, five grandchildren, and two dogs – Charlie and Benji – who think they own our home.

Also by Edward A. Dreyfus

Fiction

Shattered Direction (2016)

Gag Rule (2016)

The Midnight Shrink (2015)

Buddies (2014)

Mickey and the Plow Horse (2014)

Non-fiction

Living Life from the Inside Out (2011)

Keeping Your Sanity (2003)

Someone Right for You (2003)

Adolescence: Theory and Experience (1976)

Youth: Search for Meaning (1972)